DM13

BODIE: TRACKDOWN

Bodie was a bounty-hunter, a legalised killer. He was a survivor in a tough world where a gunman's life depended on his ruthlessness and his speed on the draw. For Bodie, killing was a trade and he was on hire to anyone with enough money and desperation. One man tried to take Bodie for a two-bit greenhorn — but Bodie wasn't about to be taken . . .

NEIL HUNTER

BODIE: TRACKDOWN

Complete and Unabridged

LINFORD
Leicester

First published in Great Britain in 1979

First Linford Edition
published April 1993

British Library CIP Data

Hunter, Neil
 Bodie the stalker no.1: trackdown.
 —Large print ed.—Linford western library
I. Title II. Series
823.914 [F]

ISBN 0–7089–7316–7

Published by
F. A. Thorpe (Publishing) Ltd.
Anstey, Leicestershire

Set by Words & Graphics Ltd.
Anstey, Leicestershire
Printed and bound in Great Britain by
T. J. Press (Padstow) Ltd., Padstow, Cornwall

For Andrew Marc and Sarah Kate —
who make the sun rise and set

1

"LEO, I reckon it's time we moved on!"

Giving a hitch to his sagging pants Leo Brack half turned to stare at the speaker. Jud Ventry, lounging on a tipped-back chair, his broad shoulders braced against the scarred wall of the adobe-built cantina, scrubbed a big hand across his stubbled jaw.

"Trouble with you, Jud, is those damn itchy feet," Brack said. He turned back to gaze out across the dusty plaza of the isolated border town, watching without much interest as a skinny dog wandered aimlessly from one patch of shadow to another, trying to find a cool place to rest. "So what's wrong with this place of a sudden?"

"Ain't a thing left worth havin'," Ventry grumbled. "Hell, Leo, I done tasted all the liquor an' screwed all

1

the women! All that leaves is water to drink and the men to take to bed — an' I ain't lookin' forward to either of those things!"

Brack fished a thin, black Mexican cigar from his pocket. Sticking it between his dry lips he searched for a match, struck it on his boot heel, and lit up. Blowing out a cloud of blue smoke he eyed Ventry's motionless fingers.

"So where do you want to go?"

Ventry eased his tilted hat away from his eyes, flicking a buzzing fly from his upper lip. "South," he said. "Over the border. See if we can find us a place with some life."

"Mexico?" Brack laughed. "I should've known. Can't go for long without getting your balls tickled by them Spanish tails, can you, Leo?"

"Man needs a hobby," Ventry insisted.

"Trouble with your damn hobby is the goddamn cost," Brack pointed out. "We're going to need a sight more money than we got now."

"So we'll take another bank," Ventry answered, as if he was talking to a child. He let his chair settle back to the ground. "You do remember what a bank is — don't you?" he asked dryly.

"One of them places where folk leave their money for us to take when we're short. Ain't that right, Jud?"

The speaker was the third member of the group. He had been sitting just inside the door of the cantina. Now he moved out into the savage glare of the hot sun, squinting his eyes against the brightness. He was young, lean and long legged. His thick blond hair hung shaggy and unruly to his shoulders.

"See," Ventry said. "Gil ain't forgotten."

Brack scowled. "You two are about as funny as a .45 slug up the ass! When you figure you've had enough laughs let's talk this out. Takin' another bank so soon after the one at Creel ain't too clever. Ain't been long enough for folk to have calmed down yet. We could walk in on some place where every son of a bitch is jittery enough to start shootin' 'fore we can get control."

"We can handle things," Gil Lutz crowed airily.

Brack rounded on him angrily. "You can quit that kind of asshole talk! Last thing I need when I take a bank is a gun-happy kid siding me who figures he's the best thing ever invented since the tail 'tween a woman's legs!"

Lutz flushed nervously. "Hell, Leo, I only said . . . "

"I know what you was aimin' to say." Brack dragged off his hat and rubbed the back of his hand across his sweaty face. "Why is it you kids got to go round provin' how damn good you are? It's that kind of asshole foolin' round that's liable to get you a nasty big hole blowed clear through you! See how tough you are then, boy, when you're crawlin' in the dirt with your insides hanging down your shirt front!"

Lutz dragged his gaze from Brack,

turning to Ventry for some kind of support. But Ventry wore an even sterner expression than Brack, and Lutz realised he'd overstepped the mark. Brack and Ventry had been riding together for a long time. They were hard, experienced men, who lived on their wits and the ability to use the guns they carried well.

"In this business," Ventry said, "when a man has a partner, he's got to know he can trust that partner with his life. He can't walk in to take some bank if his mind ain't full on the job. If he's worried about how his partner's going to act then he might as well not bother, cause sooner or later that partner's going to let him down. You remember that, Gil, cause it works for you and against you."

Lutz, feeling less than human, nodded. He didn't say another word because he couldn't trust himself to say the right thing. Instead he turned away, staring blindly up the dusty street, out towards the far end of town.

And that was when he saw the rider coming in from the sun-bleached emptiness out beyond the town limits. He stood and watched the rider for a few seconds. Then he found his voice again.

"Rider coming in!"

Ventry did no more than turn his head, narrowing his eyes against the reflected glare of the sun.

Brack, always the more nervous, walked by Lutz and stood watching the rider's approach.

"Leo?" Ventry asked after a while.

Brack simply shrugged, indicating that he did not recognise the rider.

"Probably some drifter just passing through," Ventry offered.

Brack cleared his throat and spat into the dust. "I knowd a lot of men who got killed on maybes!"

"Gil, fetch my rifle," Ventry said. He rose to his feet, unwinding his long frame slowly. He moved to stand alongside Brack as Lutz vanished inside the cantina. They stood side by side, studying the rider who was now coming along the street.

"Shit, I reckon I know that feller," Brack muttered. He began to rub the side of his nose with the tip of his left thumb, a habit he indulged in when he was thinking.

Ventry took a couple of steps forward, peering intently in the direction of the oncoming rider. A frown creased his brow. Then he gave an angry curse.

Brack glanced at him. "What?"

"Trust our bloody luck!"

"Leo?"

"It's Bodie!" Ventry stated flatly.

"Who's Bodie?" Lutz asked as he emerged from the cantina with Ventry's rifle.

Snatching the weapon from him, Ventry snapped: "Stay around, boy, and you'll find out."

"Find out what?"

"That Bodie is the best there is in his line of business. I hope you heard me cause I might not have the chance to say it again."

7

"What business?"

"The huntin' business, boy," Brack grumbled through clenched teeth. "Manhunting business! And we're the ones he's huntin' for this time!"

Lutz felt his guts coil up tight and a sick feeling began to fill his stomach.

"Hell, Leo, it's Bodie all right," Brack said suddenly.

"What's he going to do?" Lutz asked as the rider reined in his horse across the street and stepped down from the saddle.

"Do, boy?" Ventry hissed savagely. "What the hell do you think he's going to do!" He worked the lever on his rifle with a vicious jerk, forcing a round into the breech.

Lutz felt himself backing off, stepping away from Ventry and Brack. The awful realisation had hit him. Any moment now the roar of gunfire would split the empty silence, and someone would die. Gil Lutz became aware of how little he'd done in his young life, and the possibility of that life being ended here on this dusty street, in this godforsaken little town, held little appeal. The thought flitted across his mind that he'd been a fool to join up with Ventry and Brack. All right, they had shown him a good time. He'd had women. Drink. Money. But there had also been a lot of hard riding. Staying away from towns, real towns, and having to hide away in fly-infested places like this one. And all for what? The couple of thousand dollars they'd got from that bank in Creel. That had been Lutz's first job. Christ had he been scared! Waiting outside the bank with the horses while Ventry and Brack went inside. Then the silence. The seemingly eternal, empty, waiting silence. He'd begun to wonder if something had gone wrong. Sweat pouring down his face. Hands trembling as they had held the reins of the restless horses. And then the sudden eruption of gunfire that blasted the peaceful calm of Creel wide open. Ventry and Brack emerging from the bank, guns firing, canvas bags clutched in their free hands. A momentary confusion while they had struggled to get on their horses, and then the wild, uncontrolled flight through town, out across the sun-bleached terrain, hoping they could lose themselves in the silent, vaulted wilderness of that desolate landscape. For three days they had ridden almost non-stop, fearing pursuit, hardly daring to take time to rest. Finally, exhausted, they had taken refuge here in this nameless place close to the border. The town had offered little. A couple of grubby cantinas, one offering rooms for rent. Just along the street from the cantina they were using was a whorehouse run by a greasy, cold-eyed monster of a woman. She had six girls working for her, every one of them as hard as stone and just as devoid of feeling. The town had little else. A couple of stores, one of the worst eating-houses imaginable. There wasn't any law, nor did the place have a doctor. All it did have were the basic requirements afforded by a place such as this. It was a stopover. A place for drifters and fugitives to rest, or hide, before they moved to new ground. The transients who visited the town were of a kind. Always unsettled. Always wary. Always looking over their shoulders, and all, without exception, waiting for and dreading the day when somebody finally did catch up with them . . .

"Leo?" Ventry spoke softly to his partner.

Brack nodded, beginning to edge away. "Call it when you're ready," he said to Ventry.

Gil Lutz felt the hot, crumbling adobe of the cantina wall at his back. He stayed exactly where he was, a silent, unwilling spectator to the deadly game being played. Despite the fear being generated by his awareness of the unavoidable climax of the moment, Lutz found he was transfixed. He could not have taken his eyes off the three men on the dusty street for a wagonload of pure gold.

His gaze was drawn ultimately to the

11

man called Bodie. He was close enough now so that Lutz could see him clearly. Bodie was a tall man, well over six feet, with the loose gait of a lifelong horseman. He didn't appear to possess more than an average build, but that was more deception than fact. There was strength in the broad shoulders, a supple power, poised to explode. Bodie obviously allowed himself no pretensions. There was none of the usual façade of the extrovert gunman. His clothing was strictly functional. Faded levis worn over scuffed, yet cared-for boots. A dark wool shirt and a black hat that had seen better days, its wide brim curled. That hat was pulled low to shade Bodie's keen eyes, leaving much of his strong-boned face in shadow. Around his lean waist was a simple cartridge belt supporting a shaped holster. Resting in the holster was a standard 1875 model single-action Colt with plain wood grips. Bodie's right hand hung close to the butt of the Colt as he drew himself to a halt some twenty feet from Ventry and Brack. He looked like a man with all the time in the world, and he scared the hell out of Gil Lutz.

"Well?" Jud Ventry asked.

"Bank in Creel offered a thousand apiece for you boys. Dead or alive!"

Ventry spat in disgust. "And if you take us back alive we get to hang anyway? Right, Bodie?"

"You play the game, you have to follow the rules," Bodie replied.

There was a long, strained silence. Brack gave an abrupt, hollow laugh, a product of his nervousness. He wiped the back of his hand across his dry mouth.

"Hell, no!"

Jud Ventry screamed out the words, and in the same instant broke off to the left, swinging up the rifle he was holding. Slightly behind his partner in reacting, Brack snatched at the heavy Colt on his hip, starting to run forward, toward Bodie.

The manhunter moved with controlled

slowness, but there was a deliberate intent behind his actions. His Colt came out of its holster easily and was up and cocked while Brack was still clearing his weapon. Bodie turned sideways on, presenting a slimmer target, his right arm lifting the Colt in a smooth, easy motion.

Ventry, who had begun the action, was the first to fire. But he was on the move and using a rifle. His Winchester blasted a gout of flame and smoke. The bullet whacked a ragged hole in the hard earth inches away from Bodie's left boot.

"Take him, Leo!" Ventry yelled, jerking the lever of his rifle.

They were the last words he ever uttered, Bodie's Colt exploded with sound. Two shots, so close they merged into one continuous blast. The first hit Jud Ventry in the chest, punching a jagged hole that spurted blood in a bright stream. The second bullet caught him just below the left eye, ripping through flesh and

14

bone, then emerged just behind the left ear, spraying blood and bits of mangled flesh and bone. Ventry gave a hoarse grunt, twisting round on his left heel, facing in Lutz's direction. For a long moment he remained there, blood gushing from the hole in his chest and the even more hideous wound in his face. And then he pitched face down in the bloody dust, his body twitching and jerking in a final spasm of silent agony.

Before Ventry had hit the ground Bodie had swung away from him, dropping to a crouch, firing up at Leo Brack's moving figure. Bodie's gun blasted before Brack had time to cock his weapon. He shot Brack's left leg from under him, the bullet shattering Brack's kneecap in a gory flood of ruined flesh and splintered bone. Brack screamed as he went down. He smashed face first to the ground, his body arching in pain. Blood streamed from his crushed nose and lips as he struggled to raise himself,

15

still clinging to the Colt in his hand. He had the hammer halfway back when Bodie put another bullet into his body. The heavy .45 calibre bullet drove deep into Brack's chest, ripping the heart open. Brack shuddered in agony. He twisted over onto his back. Terrible choking sounds came from him as he lay kicking against the pain. Blood rose and burst from his straining lips in a red flood. It soaked his clothing, splashing to the dusty earth where it was greedily swallowed.

Gil Lutz watched the man called Bodie move towards him. There was a terrible expression on the face of the manhunter. Lutz felt a rising sickness fill his throat. Bodie was going to kill him too! Complete panic took over. Lutz thrust himself away from the wall of the cantina, eyes flicking wildly back and forth as he sought a way of escape — but he was in a trap with no way out.

"Leave me alone!" he screamed in his fear, feeling the sudden warm flood of wetness in his groin as he lost control of his bladder. "For Christ's sake leave me alone!"

Even in his panic he was aware of Bodie's abrupt move. He saw the man's arm come up. The thought flashed through his mind: He's going to shoot me! He's going to kill me! And Lutz grabbed wildly for his own gun, yanking it from the holster. He was still staring at Bodie, still seeing that raised arm, but in his fear, his total panic, he failed to digest the fact that it was Bodie's left arm. Not the right. Not the gun arm. As far as Lutz was concerned he had seconds in which to defend himself and he reacted in the only way he knew. He brought up his gun, thumb dragging back the hammer, bringing the muzzle round to line up on Bodie.

"Damn you, boy, don't!"

Bodie's plea was lost on Lutz. He was too far gone with fear. Too committed to draw back. He triggered a single, frantic shot, not bothering to see where it had gone before he started to cock his gun again for the second shot — which he never made.

There were two bullets left in Bodie's gun. He put them both into Lutz's lean body, and the range was so close that Lutz was lifted off his feet and tossed across the street like a rag doll. His gory wounds exposed splintered white rib bones. In his dying moments Lutz felt blood fill his mouth and nose. He coughed harshly, feeling the blood spray from his lips in a frothy mist. He began to crawl blindly across the street, tearing out his nails as he clawed at the hard earth. He didn't know where he was going or why, but he didn't want to just lie there. So he crawled, leaving behind a slimy trail of blood in the pale dust of that nameless town in the middle of nowhere. And that was where he died.

The man named Bodie put away his gun after he had reloaded it. He stood and surveyed the three bloody corpses. Glancing at the twisted body of the boy he shook his head. There hadn't been a need for him to die. Damn fool! If only he'd listened before he'd started shooting. All Bodie had wanted to tell him was that the 'Dead or Alive' notice had only been for Ventry and Brack. The boy, Lutz, would have got away with no more than a few years behind bars. He could have come out a free man with a chance to start again. But Lutz had chosen his own way and he paid for it. Maybe his actions had been fired by pure fear. By panic. The motivation didn't make that much difference to Bodie. He could be killed just as easily by a bullet from a madman as from one coming out of the gun of a professional killer. Bodie had long ago ceased to make any distinction. He had a simple, hard-and-fast rule, and he never wavered from it. If somebody, anybody, pointed a gun his way, with the intention of using it, then that person had better be damn fast and sure, because Bodie wasn't about to give away any free tries. It was a good rule. It was a wise rule. In his line of business it was the only rule. It was the reason Bodie was still alive, and a lot of other men were dead and buried and forgotten.

Bodie made his way towards the cantina. Cautious faces were starting to show themselves. All he wanted from them was the whereabouts of the horses belonging to the three dead outlaws. Bodie was going to need the horses if he wanted to haul the corpses back to Creel. It was what he had to do if he wanted to collect the bounty offered by the bank, and he hadn't come all this way just for the exercise.

2

IT took Bodie five days to make the return journey to Creel. He arrived mid-morning on a hot day and the stench from the three corpses, each one wrapped in a blanket and draped over the back of a horse, hovered over him like some virulent plague. He led his grisly burdens up the main street, ignoring the staring citizens, his ears closed to the protests at his bringing such terrible things into town. Bodie rode up to the stonebuilt jail, easing himself from the saddle and tethering his horse. Creel's lawman came out of his office to see what all the fuss was about. He took one look at Bodie and decided not to get too involved himself. The marshal knew Bodie's reputation. He also knew about Bodie's quick temper. The manhunter had a reputation for violence that was hard to beat. Only a fool would deliberately rouse Bodie's temper.

"Ventry and Brack?" the marshal asked.

Bodie simply nodded. "Third one's the kid. Lutz. He didn't want to listen to what I had to tell him. If he had he'd be sitting that saddle instead of draped over it."

The marshal rubbed his chin. "Could be bad news there," he said. "Gil Lutz had four brothers. They run a spread north of town. Bodie, they're a hard bunch. It ain't going to sit right with them when they hear you brought Gil back dead."

Bodie had already stepped up on the boardwalk. He made his way inside the jail. The marshal instructed his deputy to take the bodies over to the undertakers, then followed Bodie inside. Closing the door the marshal went across to the small stove in the corner and poured out two mugs of coffee. He handed one to Bodie before sitting down behind his desk.

"Bodie, I'm not telling you to get out of Creel," the marshal began. "You haven't broken any laws. All I'm saying is, why stick around if there's a chance of trouble with the Lutz boys?"

Bodie tasted the coffee. "Marshal, you make good coffee but you give lousy advice. One thing I've never done is back off from trouble. I can't afford to. Once folk start to figure I'm going soft I'll be out of work. If the Lutz boys start trouble they'll get it back. Right now all I want to do is collect my money and get myself a room at the hotel. I want a bath and a shave and some clean clothes. After that I figure to eat. Then I'll decide what to do next."

The marshal sighed. He should have known better than to try and talk Bodie into leaving town. He had a feeling that Creel was going to have problems if Bodie stayed long. Yet he very seldom went out of his way to initiate that violence. There were always others ready to do that. It was said that Bodie had a lot of enemies. It was a fact that he had buried a great number of them. He was known to be a hard, no-nonsense man. A man not to be taken lightly.

"I'll get the paperwork sorted out and have the money for you in about an hour." The marshal emptied his mug. "You going over to the hotel?"

Bodie nodded. "Yeah. I might as well wait in comfort for my money."

The crowd of onlookers had drifted away by the time Bodie emerged from the jail. His horse stood alone at the hitching rail. Bodie took the reins and led the animal along the street, to a livery stable. The establishment was run by a wizened old man with grey hair and fierce blue eyes. He nodded as Bodie brought his animal inside.

"Hear you got them bastards who took the bank," the old man said. His name was Greensburgh. He'd been in the territory for longer than anyone could recall. It was said that when he had first arrived there was nothing but wide open spaces, Indians, and buffalo. Greensburgh had survived and he had watched the country grow. He was as hard now as he had been in his youth, and had a low opinion of the so-called civilising of the country. "Blown 'em all to hell by what I hear. Shootin's too good for them useless tramps."

"They wanted it that way," Bodie said. He led his horse to an empty stall and unsaddled. He forked in some fresh straw and filled the water and grain boxes for the animal.

Greensburgh watched the operation silently, puffing on an old pipe stuck in one corner of his mouth. "Man who looks after his horse can't be all bad," he remarked finally.

"Knowing I got your approval, old man, is going to help me sleep tonight," Bodie said.

A dry chuckle rose in Greensburgh's throat. "Bodie, I like you!"

Slinging his saddlebags over one shoulder, Bodie picked up his rifle and headed for the door. "You look after that horse, else you might have reason to change your mind."

"Don't you fret none, boy. I'll take care of him." At the door of the stable the old man cleared his throat. "Hey, Bodie, keep your eyes skinned for them Lutz boys. They get to hear what happened to that youngster . . . well, I guess you already been told how they are."

"Yeah, I heard."

"The Lutzs, they come from way back. Tennessee mountain folk. Got this thing about family ties. They got long memories and hate pretty fierce."

Bodie didn't say anything. He started along the street. After a few steps he glanced back over his shoulder. Greensburgh was still watching him.

"Take care of the horse, Mr Greensburgh."

The old man nodded. "Will do, boy, and you're purely welcome."

Bodie walked uptown and went inside the 'Creel House', the town's best hotel. It was obvious that it was

26

Creel's best establishment because it had carpet in the lobby, clean paint on the walls, and the magazines left around for patrons to read were no more than two months old. Bodie crossed to the desk, put down his rifle and spun the register to sign in.

"No need for that, Mr Bodie," the desk clerk said. He was a slender, pale man. His dark hair was plastered to his skull like a cap and he wore a thin moustache on his upper lip. He beamed across the desk at Bodie, clasping his thin, white hands together.

"Why?" Bodie asked, his tone indicating that he required a straight answer.

The clerk reached below the desk and withdrew a long buff envelope. He handed it to Bodie, who saw that his name was written on the front. Bodie opened the envelope and took out the folded notepaper. A new, crisp, $500 bill was inside the paper, and written on the expensive surface of the paper was a short message: Mister Bodie, please find enclosed a $500 retainer. This is for half an hour of your time. It could be worth 10,000 dollars if you agree to my proposition. You room is booked and anything you require. I will be in touch. Lyle Trask.

"Is this the Lyle Trask I think it is?" Bodie asked the clerk.

"*The* Mr Trask," the clerk affirmed.

Bodie read the note again. His curiosity was aroused by the short but tempting message. After a moment he came to a decision. He pocketed the note and the money.

"Let me have the key," he told the clerk. "I want hot water for a bath and send somebody up who can go and get me some clean clothes."

"Certainly, Mr Bodie," the clerk beamed. "Anything you need, don't hesitate to ask."

"How about a girl? Young. Good looking. Experienced but not too much?"

The clerk's face took on a shocked expression. He touched the tips of

28

his fingers to his thin lips. Then he managed a weak smile. "Mr Bodie is having his little joke of course?" The tail end of the sentence was almost a plea.

Bodie picked up the key and his rifle, turning to go upstairs. He glanced at the clerk. "Sure," he said. "Mr Bodie is just having a little joke." As he climbed the stairs Bodie wondered for a moment what the clerk would have done if Mr Bodie had not been joking. Knowing who was behind all the grand treatment being showered on him, there would probably have been a girl delivered to his room within a short time, and no questions asked.

The room turned out to be the best in the hotel. A double room, overlooking the street, with a separate bathroom and lounge. Bodie dropped his saddlebags beside the huge bed, regretting with every passing second the fact that there wasn't a woman on tap. He took off his gunbelt and hung it from one of the bedposts. Sitting down

29

in one of the plush armchairs he took out the note and read it again.

Now what would Lyle Trask want from him? He knew of Trask. Then again, who hadn't. Lyle Trask was one of the wealthiest businessmen in this part of southwest Texas. He had holdings in every kind of money-making operation. Trask owned cattle by the thousand. He bred horses. There was a stageline that ran under his banner. He even owned a railroad. His shipping and freight companies reached far and wide. Bodie was certain that the man even had banking interests. Lyle Trask, in fact, was a tycoon. A hard-dealing, fast-thinking, powerful operator. He had worked his way up from nothing, his first dealings being undertaken while he was still in his twenties. Now he was somewhere in his early forties, comparatively young for his breed, and it seemed as if nothing could stop him becoming even more powerful, and more wealthy. So what did a man of Lyle Trask's position want with Bodie? Bodie's business was violence and sudden death. His tools were his rifle and his handgun. The more he thought about it the more intrigued Bodie became.

He was still turning the matter over in his mind a couple of hours later when he left his room and went downstairs. It was close to lunchtime and Bodie was hungry. The ragged, unshaven Bodie had gone. Bathed and shaved, dressed in a new dark suit, with a white shirt and dark string tie, Bodie felt human again. The only reminders of his former appearance were his hat and the gunbelt he had strapped on under the coat of his suit.

The hotel had its own dining room. Bodie was shown a private table situated in front of the window, looking out on the street. He ordered a large steak with all the trimmings, a bottle of wine, and a pot of coffee. While he waited for his meal Bodie sat back and watched Creel go about its business.

He could see the jail from where

he was sitting, and just as his meal
arrived, Bodie observed four horsemen
come along the street and rein in at
the jail. There was something familiar
about the four roughly dressed, heavily-
armed riders. Bodie watched them step
up on the boardwalk and go inside the
jail. He drew his gaze from the window
and set to eating his meal. It was only
as he was drinking his second cup of
coffee that it came to him.

Gil Lutz!

That was who the four men had
reminded him of. And he realised
who the four must be. Bodie glanced
through the window towards the jail,
but the four horses had gone. He
leaned back in his seat, pouring himself
more coffee. He made no attempt to
cut short his meal. He was not in any
kind of hurry.

A face Bodie knew appeared at
his table. Creel's marshal. He looked
worried. He thrust a thick envelope at
Bodie.

"Got your money," he said. Beads

of sweat gleamed on his face.

"Wasn't any need for you to bring it," Bodie said. "I was going to come over to see you when I finished."

"Look, Bodie . . . " the marshal began.

"I was you, I'd sit down before I fell down."

The marshal slid into the seat facing Bodie.

"You want a drink or something?" Bodie asked. The marshal shook his head. "Marshal, I know what's worrying you. I saw the Lutz boys ride in a while back."

"You didn't hear what they had to say, though! Did you?" The marshal's voice rose slightly in his excitement. "Hell, Bodie, I thought they were going to shoot me!"

Bodie glanced over the rim of his coffee cup. "Why? You do something to upset them?"

"This ain't funny, Bodie!" The marshal looked around as other diners glanced his way. Lowering his voice he said: "It's like I told you, Bodie. Killing that kid was bound to bring you trouble! And it has! Jesus, man, they're out there and they aim to blow you apart!"

Bodie poured the last of the coffee into his cup. He spooned in sugar, slowly and deliberately.

"Damn you, Bodie, is that all you care. Four men lookin' to blow you from hell to breakfast an' all you can do is drink coffee!"

"One thing I ain't about to do is leave town. I've got business here in Creel. If those Lutz boys come looking for me, they better be faster than the kid I brought in hanging face down over the saddle."

"So what do you aim to do?" the marshal asked.

Bodie grinned at him. It was a grin of a wolf anticipating its prey. "Me? Not a damn thing! Unless somebody else starts it!"

The marshal stood up. He felt completely useless. His hands were tied and he knew it. Bodie was in the clear as far as the law was concerned. He hadn't done a thing out of place, nor would he. If the Lutz boys pushed matters as far as a gunfight, which they most certainly would, then Bodie could kill them and no court could touch him. In a way the marshal was glad that was the way it would turn out. He didn't want to be in the position of trying to arrest Bodie. He would sooner turn in his badge. Better to be out of work than dead!

Bodie watched the marshal leaving the dining room. He finished his coffee and left himself. Crossing to the desk he gestured to the clerk.

"Did Trask say when he'd be in Creel?" Bodie asked.

The clerk shook his head. "No, sir, Mister Trask refrained from giving that information."

Bodie put his hat on and walked out of the hotel. It was almost one o'clock. Creel was at lunch. The street was practically deserted. Most of the stores had closed for the hour. Bodie heard music coming from a saloon just up the street and decided to take a walk. There might be a poker game in progress he could sit in on. He cut across the street, aware of his exposed position, but also keeping a keen eye open for any unusual moves being made. He reached the saloon without trouble and went inside.

As the doors swung shut behind him Bodie came to a dead stop just inside. Sitting at one of the tables, a half-empty bottle on the table top, were the four Lutz brothers.

One of them glanced up as Bodie entered the saloon. He nudged the others and said something. The other brothers turned to look at Bodie.

Bodie ignored them and crossed to the bar. He found a space and gestured to the bartender.

"Beer," Bodie said.

The bartender brought the beer in a large, thick glass which he placed in front of Bodie. There was an odd expression on the man's face and his gaze moved constantly from Bodie to the table where the Lutz brothers were sitting.

"Something troubling you, feller?" Bodie asked.

The bartender shook his head quickly, muttering a denial, and moved to the far end of the bar where he began to polish already clean glasses as though his life depended on it.

Bodie drank his beer. Behind him he could hear subdued talk coming from the Lutz's table. He ignored it. But he remained aware of their presence. And when one of the brothers uttered angry words, Bodie tensed, and waited. A chair scraped against the wooden floor as it was hurriedly shoved back.

"Spending your blood money, Bodie? How does it feel getting paid for murdering kids?"

Bodie turned slowly. He leaned against the bar, still holding his glass of beer and stared coldly at the man standing before him.

"The kid died because he pulled a gun on me. If he'd waited a while I would have told him the 'Dead or Alive' notice was only for Ventry and Brack. He didn't want to listen. That was his mistake."

The man shook his head savagely. "The hell you say! You gunned him down, Bodie! A goddam kid, that was all!"

"If he was a kid he shouldn't have been playing a man's game. Mister, I don't give a shit about whose brother he was. He was in on that bank raid and he was riding with Ventry and Brack. Seems to me if you reckon to care for him, how come you let him team up with that pair in the first place?"

The man gave out a roar. He half-turned, throwing a glance at his three brothers. "Now he's says it's our fault! For Christ sake, let's get on with what we come for . . . "

"You sure there's enough of you to

handle it?" Bodie asked, a taunting edge to his tone.

The man swung round to face Bodie again, his face dark with rage. His lips peeled back to expose his stained teeth. Allowing his pent-up emotions to get the better of him, he launched a powerful swing to Bodie's face.

Bodie eased his body to one side and the heavy fist slid by his face. The force behind the blow pulled the man in closer to Bodie. Before the man could recover his balance Bodie drove the thick glass into his face. It struck with a meaty thwack, shattering on impact. The broken glass tore open the man's jaw and cheek. Soft flesh was sliced apart. Blood gushed from the deep gashes and the man let out a terrified scream of pain. He clutched at his bloody face, stumbling forward against Bodie who shoved him aside, turning to face the oncoming three Lutz brothers. They rushed at him in an uncoordinated bunch, their actions fired by anger, which drove them to reckless violence. The one in the lead drove a wild punch at Bodie's face that caught him across the left cheek, splitting the flesh. Before the man could follow with a second blow Bodie caught hold of his shirt front, yanking the man off balance. Dragging him forwards and down Bodie smashed the man head-first against the edge of the bar. The man's cry of pain was reduced to a choked whimper as his face crushed against the hard wood. There was a sodden crunch as his nose was reduced to a pulpy mass. Strong hands grabbed Bodie's left arm, swinging him away from the bar. A solid blow clouted him across the side of the skull. Bodie slid back against the bar, shaking his head to clear away the muzzy pain. He saw a distorted, angry face lunging at him, was aware of another one close by. He sensed the coming blow aimed at his face and let himself drop to a crouch. Then he lunged forward, smashing his hard shoulder into the closest groin. He heard a man scream in pain. Bodie shoved hard, lifting as he moved forward. He felt the man's feet leave the floor. Bodie used his hands to accelerate the movement of the squirming body. The yelling man was thrown over Bodie's shoulder to the saloon floor. He hit with a crippling impact, twisting over onto his back, gasping for air through paralysed lungs. Turning, Bodie spotted the man trying to sit up. He lashed out with his right foot, opening a long gash that started to bleed heavily. Something cracked sharply across the side of Bodie's skull. He stumbled and went down on one knee. Hot blood began to stream down the side of his face. He threw a quick glance in the direction the blow had come from and saw the remaining Lutz coming at him again. The man had a whisky bottle in his hand and he was swinging it at Bodie again. Bodie threw up his left arm to block the blow. The bottle struck his arm over the bone, pain flaring the length of the limb.

Bodie kicked out with his left foot, the heel of his boot driving against the man's right knee. Bone cracked with an audible sound.

Bodie twisted his body away from the bar, starting to rise to his feet. For a drawn-out moment the saloon was devoid of sound. Almost to his feet Bodie caught the faint double-click of a gun being cocked. He reacted instinctively, placing the sound as he threw himself across the floor. Even as he allowed his body to roll he was snatching his Colt from its holster, thumb dogging back the hammer, bringing the gun round on its target.

The other man's gun blasted first. The bullet hit the floor where Bodie's body should have been. It ripped up a long sliver of wood. Then Bodie triggered his first shot. He saw the bullet strike the man in the chest. It slammed him back against the bar where he threw out his left arm, grasping the edge of the bar to hold himself on his feet. His face was twisted in pain. Blood burst from the wound and soaked the front of his grubby shirt. Even so the man tried to loose off another shot. This time Bodie shot first. His bullet, ripped its way through his skull and tore off the top of his head on its way out.

There was a scramble of noise off to Bodie's right. He jerked his head round in time to see one of the Lutz brother's roll across the top of the bar and vanish from sight behind it. There was a sudden splintering of glass, followed by the oiled click of gun-hammers being eared back. Realisation hit Bodie with the force of cold water in the face. The bartender's scattergun! Most probably a sawn-off double-barrel shotgun loaded with heavy shot. A deadly, close-quarter weapon with devastating power. Bodie didn't wait. He judged where the man was behind the bar and put two shots through the panelling. There was a yell of pain.

"Son of a bitch! Here's yours, Bodie!"

The man came up yelling, taking an instant to locate Bodie, then more precious seconds as he attempted to line up the shotgun. Bodie didn't wait. Held two-handed, his Colt blossomed flame and smoke as he fired. His bullet took the man between the eyes, blasting a fist-sized hole in the back of the skull. Blood and brains and hair-matted flesh clung to the mirror behind the bar. As he fell back the hit man's fingers jerked the triggers on the shotgun. Both barrels erupted with a solid crash of sound. The double-charge gouged the polished top of the bar, then struck one of the Lutz brothers who was climbing painfully to his feet. The man received the spreading charge in the face and chest. His lacerated body, streaming blood from the terrible wounds, was thrown across the saloon floor, where he lay flopping around in agony, his blood spreading across the dirty floor in long, bright fingers.

Bodie climbed slowly to his feet. He touched his fingers to his bleeding cheek. Deep stabs of pain began to flare over his body. He heard somebody groan. It was the man he had hit with the beer glass. He was slumped at the base of the bar, bloody hands cupped against his face. Congealing blood hung from his hands in thin streams.

The saloon doors burst open. The marshal stepped inside. He stared round the silent saloon, shaking his head at the bloody state of the place. His gaze finally came to rest on Bodie as the man walked across the saloon towards him. Bodie looked a mess. There was blood down one side of his face, more of it soaking his coat and shirt. His Colt was still in his right hand. The marshal was on the verge of saying something when he caught sight of the look in Bodie's eyes. A cold sensation grew in the marshal's gut and he remained silent. He never knew just how close he had come to dying at that moment. Bodie had made himself a promise that if the marshal so much as uttered one word, he would use the remaining bullet in his gun to blow the man's brains out.

And Bodie always kept his promises. Especially the ones he made to himself!

3

LYLE TRASK arrived two days later. By then Creel had worn out its excitement over the bloody gunfight between the Lutz brothers and the man called Bodie. It wasn't as if the Lutz clan had been very popular anyway, people were quick to point out. A hard bunch of greasysackers, more than one opinion determined. The dead Lutz brothers were quickly buried. The wounded one had his face sewn up and returned to the ranch to recover and to brood in silence. The town of Creel talked the subject out and returned to normal. The only physical reminder of the incident was the lone, silent figure of Bodie. He went about his business, bothered no one, and expected to receive the same treatment. He got it, because nobody in Creel had any desire to become involved with the man who had taken on the four Lutz brothers and walked away with no more than a couple of bruises and a cut cheek.

Precisely at noon, Lyle Trask's private train pulled in to Creels' tiny depot, shunted onto the short spurline running beside the main track, and waited in solitary splendour while one of Trask's minions walked up into town to summon Bodie.

Bodie was in the hotel dining room eating his lunch. He listened in silence to what Trask's man had to say, then carried on eating.

"Don't you understand what I'm saying?" the man snapped. He was a hard faced, cold-eyed individual, dressed in a well cut grey suit. His shirt was white, starched. Short cut dark hair clung tightly to his square head like a cap. "Mr Trask wants to see you now, Bodie!"

Bodie sighed. He put down his fork, swallowed the meat he was chewing, and raised his eyes to meet those of Trask's man.

"You ain't talkin' to Trask now, sonny, so don't try to impress me how tough you think you are. Now, you've passed on your message. I suggest you trot off back to Trask, tell him how clever you've been, and go sit in a corner until he tosses you a bone. That'll give me time to finish my meal before I come to see him."

"The hell I will, you son of a b . . . !" The man's hand moved towards the gun he wore in a shoulder-holster.

"Be sure you're going to kill me if you pull that thing out," Bodie said evenly, "because the minute I see it I'm going to blow your goddam brains all over this room!"

The man hesitated, staring fixedly at Bodie, and realising that he was going to be in trouble if he carried the matter further. He let his hand ease away from his coat. What the hell, he thought, I've done what Trask ordered. I've given Bodie the message, it's up to him now. He backed off a couple of steps, turned abruptly and strode out of the dining room and on out of the hotel. It was only when he paused on the boardwalk that he became aware of the sweat beading his face. He pulled a handkerchief out of his pocket and wiped his face angrily. Though he would never have admitted it to a living soul, the man called Bodie scared the hell out of him. There was an air of menace emanating from Bodie, a silent, invisible warning and it said don't come too close, don't push too hard.

Bodie, meanwhile, carried on with his meal. His appetite had waned a little. He was angry at the minor confrontation with Trask's man. There was never any escape, he thought. No matter where a man went, there was always some hardnosed bastard trying to shoulder his way through life. They never asked, they always demanded. Never waited until something was offered, their way insisted that they took. They went through life believing they had the edge over everything and everybody — until the day the hammer fell, and then they lay back and screamed bloody murder because they had got hurt.

Finishing off his meal, Bodie left the hotel. He took a slow walk through town and as the last of Creel's buildings fell behind him, he cut off towards the rail depot. A dry wind, coming in off the flat Texas plain, lifted gritty dust that hissed through the bleached grass sprouting up between the rail ties. Bodie stepped across the main track, his eyes fixed on the squatting bulk of the train waiting on the spurline.

Trask's locomotive, gleaming in black and maroon, fronted a long, richly decorated Pullman coach. At the rear of the coach was a wide observation-platform. As Bodie neared the platform a tall Negro, wearing a white jacket, stepped through the door and stood waiting.

"Mr Trask is waiting to receive you,

sir," the Negro said.

Bodie stepped up onto the platform and followed the Negro inside. He was led through the coach. The interior was plushly decorated. Inlaid wood panels lined the walls. Thick carpet covered the floors. All the fittings were of highly polished brass. The very air was redolent of wealth, of high-living. To Bodie it was stifling. He was not impressed by the trappings Lyle Trask surrounded himself with.

The man himself was a surprise. Lyle Trask, though dressed expensively, did not completely fit with the decor. He was a tall, solidly-built man who carried his years well. Women would have called him handsome. His blond hair, framed a strong, tanned face. Blue eyes. An easy, friendly smile. He came across the coach to take Bodie's hand in a powerful grip, dismissing the Negro with a curt movement of his head.

"Sit down, Bodie. Would you like a drink? Cigar?"

Bodie sat, watching the man as he filled heavy cut-glass tumblers with fine, mellow whisky. Mr Trask, Bodie told himself, is trying too damned hard.

"Did you enjoy your lunch?" Trask asked pleasantly. He handed Bodie a glass, settling himself in a leather armchair facing his guest.

"I managed to," Bodie said.

"I'm afraid you rather upset Teal," Trask said, smiling again.

"That's tough," Bodie said. "He'll get over it. The way he acts it's something he'll have to live with. I've learned it's a fact of life, Mr Trask. You push somebody, then nine times out of ten they push back."

Trask took a drink. "The way I hear it you've been demonstrating that very philosophy yourself. I'm referring to the run in you had with the Lutz brothers."

"It would have happened sooner or later. They chose sooner," Bodie stated, his tone indicating that he had no more to say on the matter. "Mr Trask, I don't need the bullshit. If you've got business to discuss let's get to it!"

Lyle Trask's face stiffened for a fraction of a second. He revealed in that instant that he was not used to being spoken to in such a manner. He expected subservience and most probably got it from the people he employed. But he quickly covered his inner anger, telling himself that this man Bodie was not like the everyday employee who jumped at each snap of his fingers. Bodie might jump, but it would most likely be to bite the very finger snapping at him.

"Very well, Bodie let's talk business." Trask stood up and crossed to the large oak desk positioned at the far end of the coach. He picked up a sheaf of papers and returned to his armchair. Leaning forward he handed the papers to Bodie. "I'm sure you recognise those faces."

Bodie glanced through the sheaf of 'Wanted' posters. He knew them all.

"Jim Tyree. Lee Kendal. Morgan Taylor. Jesse Largo. And the leader of the bunch — Hoyt Reefer," Trask said, identifying each face as Bodie exposed it. "The authorities have been trying to get their hands on Reefer's bunch for years now. They have failed every time. Because of that failure Reefer and his gang have been free to terrorise at will. They rob and murder, they destroy what they can't use. Nothing is too risky for them. Nothing too low. I think it is time that Hoyt Reefer and his gang were wiped out. That's why I asked you here. I think you are the only man who can do it, Bodie. And I'm willing to pay you $10,000 on top of the money being offered for the gang. If you add up the various amounts you'll find the total is also $10,000. That would be 20,000 in all, Bodie. Just for delivering five dead outlaws!"

Bodie glanced up from the posters. He looked Trask in the eyes, wondering what was going on in the man's mind.

Whatever it was nothing showed in Trask's face.

"I get the feeling there was a message in the way you said 'dead outlaws'."

"You felt right, Bodie. Dead outlaws. No prisoners. Just corpses. Brought first to me."

Bodie's reaction was simple and direct. "Why?" he asked.

"Did you ever think, Bodie, that for a man like me there comes the day when I find I've reached the top? I've run out of things to buy and sell. I've built all I want to build. But I still have ambitions. One I've had for a long time. To go into politics. Right now I've reached the stage in my life where I can realise that ambition. I have the money. I have the contacts, too. And I have a certain amount of influence."

"How does Hoyt Reefer's bunch fit in?" Bodie asked, already forming a picture for himself and anxious to see if it fell in line with Trask's reasoning.

"I'm sure I don't have to enlighten

you on the need for law and order in the territory. Law enforcement agencies are having a hard time. It's a case of too many criminals, too much territory and not enough lawmen." Trask smiled apologetically. "I don't wish to appear disdainful, Bodie, but if there was enough efficient law there wouldn't be any need for your kind."

Bodie drained his whisky. "You won't hurt my feelings, Mr Trask. It's all been said before. You're all the same. You don't like me. A lot of you hate my guts. I've been called all the dirty names in the book. But when it comes right down to it, Mr Trask, you still need me. Somebody has to clean up the horseshit. Your kind don't like getting your hands dirty, so you pay me to do it for you. Trouble is you still complain about the stink. It's one of those things about horseshit — it sticks. So we've all got to put up with the smell until somebody figures out a better way to clean up the mess."

Trask refilled their whisky glasses.

Returning to his seat he leaned back against the padded rest. "A speech like that, Bodie, could get you into politics."

"No thanks," Bodie said. "Ain't no profit in changing one dirty game for another."

Trask ignored the remark. "I think by now you'll have formed a picture of why I want to hire you. When I commence my campaign for the forthcoming elections, I shall be using as my platform the need for stronger law enforcement. The territory needs to be made safe for the growing communities. Lawlessness must be put down. I intend, Bodie, to make that my prime concern. And to prove my capabilities to the voters I intend to give them Hoyt Reefer and his gang. Not alive. Not behind bars, where clever lawyers can use the law to free them so they can carry on with their brutal ways. When I offer Reefer's bunch they will be stone-cold dead. And that will mean a damn sight more to the voters

58

than all the other airy promises they've been handed so many times before."

From what he'd already heard Bodie could see Lyle Trask going far in politics. The man had the right kind of appeal. He would use the deaths of Hoyt Reefer and his gang as emotional rungs in the ladder that would lift him to the top of his particular tree. The voters would see Trask as a powerful force in the cause of law enforcement. As Trask himself had said, actions would speak louder than words. The voters would look at the dead outlaws and see physical proof of Trask's promises. Not empty air but direct results. And Trask would see to it that the whole campaign revolved around his 'bodies not boasts' election platform. Trask would stand a pretty good chance of being voted in, especially by the electorate of this part of the country. Texas had always been strong on the hardline when it came to law and order. The whole history of the territory had been one of direct action. Texans were noted for their lack of patience with the long-winded vocaliser. They would rather get on with the job themselves, being particularly aligned to the notion that actions speak louder than words. Texas was a big country. It contained few people in comparison to its size. That meant there were a lot of families who might have to ride for a couple of days before they saw their neighbour. It created self-sufficiency in every man, woman and child. Look after your own came first. And there were enough distractions to put that philosophy to the test. If it wasn't the Comanches and their Kiowa allies, it was Mexican bandits jumping the border. Then there were the white renegades, a lot of them still on the run from the war and so set in their ways they didn't know anything except stealing and raping and killing. The western expansion was creating problems too. There were range wars over grazing land. Over rights to water. The cattlemen fighting the farmers. Fighting the railroads.

Fighting each other. As Trask had said, law enforcement was a big issue, and any man who showed willing in the cause of expanding the way for peace was liable to become a popular vote-catcher. And with Trask it would only be the beginning. Once he had his foot in the door he wouldn't be happy until that door was the one to the Governor's mansion.

"Well, Bodie? Have I been wasting my time and yours?"

Bodie allowed a thin smile to curve up the corners of his mouth. "For what you're paying, Mr Trask, you can take all the time you want."

"You accept the assignment?"

"Been a fault of mine ever since the first time a girl winked at me, Mr Trask. I never have been able to resist a challenge!"

4

BODIE rode out of Creel the next morning. Once clear of town he cut off to the south. He rode for three hours, crossing the muddy ribbon of the Pecos River an hour before noon. On the far bank he rested his horse, taking time to sit in the scant shade of a few trees edging the river at the spot he'd chosen to cross. Allowing himself the luxury of a thin cigar, Bodie had digested the information Lyle Trask had given him on the most recent sighting of the Reefer gang. Three days previously, so Trask's information had revealed, a freighter named Roak had been attacked by an armed bunch of men. Roak had been shot and left for dead, his wagon and team taken by the raiders. In the wagon was a shipment of arms and ammunition intended for a store in the town of

Hayes, a small town near the Rio Grande. The shipment had consisted of fifty new Winchester repeating rifles, twenty-five Colt handguns and five-thousand rounds of ammunition. Roak, though badly shot up, had managed to reach a mall ranch. Before he had died from his wounds, the freighter gave a clear description of one of his killers. The description fitted exactly to that of Morgan Taylor, one of Hoyt Reefer's men. Roak had even mentioned the fact that the small finger on the man's left hand was missing, and Morgan Taylor had lost his finger in a shootout in Laredo during his early days with Hoyt Reefer. The local law had tried to follow the trail left by Reefer's gang, but had lost it in the foothills of the Guadalupe Mountains. That trail would be days old now, Bodie knew, but he'd followed cold trails before, and at least it was something to go on, however slight.

Moving on, he drifted south, hoping to reach Hayes by nightfall. He wanted a few words with the town's lawman. It was possible that the man might be able to give him some idea of Reefer's intended destination. It was a slight hope, but worth following up.

The day was hot. There wasn't a breath of wind. The sunbleached terrain, mainly undulating and rocky this close to the border, lay open and defenceless against the ceaseless rage of the sun. The great empty curve of the sky, blue and cloudless, shimmered gently. Bodie didn't push his horse. He let the animal make its own pace. The reward for folly out here was ultimately death. A man on foot stood little chance unless he knew the land intimately, and few men did. Bodie had as good a knowledge of this part of the country as most, maybe better than most, yet he had no desire to put that knowledge to the test.

Bringing his horse's head round Bodie put it down a sandy slope, leaning gently back in the saddle to counteract the angle of descent.

It was in that instant the shot came. A rifle firing from somewhere on his left. The bullet burned through the air a fraction of an inch from his throat. Bodie kicked his feet from the stirrups and let his body roll from the saddle. He closed his right hand over the butt of his Colt, sliding it from the holster as his shoulder struck the slope. He rolled away from his horse, dust rising in pale coils behind him. Bodie heard the rifle fire again. The bullet clipped the sleeve of his shirt. He slid to the foot of the slope, drawing his feet under him and thrust upright, eyes searching the slope above, seeking the rifleman. He had worked out the general position of his attacker. All he needed now was a definite sighting.

He got it seconds later as the rifleman showed himself, already in the process of setting up another shot. The man was halfway up the slope, part concealed behind a jutting slab of weathered stone.

Bodie threw up his Colt, squeezing

off two quick shots, then ran forwards, angling up the slope. The move took the rifleman by surprise. He'd been expecting Bodie to turn away. To retreat — not attack. Both of Bodie's bullets struck the rock and howled off into space. The rifleman lurched back a step, hurriedly readjusting his aim. Bodie, meantime took the chance to pause, level his Colt, holding for a second — then he eased back on the light trigger. The Colt cracked once, muzzle lifting. A vivid gout of red exploded from the rifleman's left shoulder. He twisted round, his rifle jerking skywards as it went off. The man lost his footing on the loose slope and slithered into view from behind his boulder.

Bodie stood yards away, waiting, his face wearing a bitter, brutal expression, as he silently watched the rifleman attempt to regain his balance while desperately trying to retrain his rifle on his intended target. The rifleman was the surviving member of the Lutz family. The one Bodie had cut up with the beer glass. One side of the man's face was swathed in white bandage. He twisted his head round and threw a murderous glance in Bodie's direction, making a further attempt to lift his rifle and fire despite the shattered shoulder.

That was when Bodie raised his Colt with deliberate intent and emptied it into Lutz's writhing body. Each bullet ripped a fresh, blood-spurting path, pulping flesh and splintering bone. Lutz pitched face first down the slope. He hit the bottom with a bone-jarring smack, humping painfully on one side. Reaching him Bodie toed him over onto his back. Lutz stared up at him through eyes already glazing over.

"Goddam you, Bodie," he hissed through bloody lips. "We should have done for you back in Creel! Backshot you like I wanted to!"

"Yeah? Well you didn't, you son of a bitch!"

Lutz made a violent effort to raise himself off the ground but only

managed to lift his head. "Sod you
. . . Bodie . . . we should have . . . took
you . . . the others . . . said we
. . . could!"

A humourless smile ghosted across
Bodie's lips. "Couple of minutes you'll
be able to tell 'em they were wrong,
feller."

Lutz watched the manhunter turn
away and walk to his waiting horse.
As Bodie mounted up Lutz screamed:
"Damnit, man ain't you goin' to help
me? I . . . ain't about . . . to . . . make
it . . . !"

Bodie glanced down at Lutz as he
rode by. "Nothing I can do, feller, even
if I had a mind to!"

"What . . . the . . . hell!" Lutz raved,
spitting out blood. "Christ, Bodie, what
. . . do you . . . expect me to do?"

"Only thing a man in your condition
can do, Lutz. I guess you lie down and
die!" Bodie said coldly, and rode on.

He closed his ears to the rantings
of the man who only minutes before
had been trying to end his life. He

recalled what the old livery stable owner — Greensburgh — had told him about the Lutz's inbred hate, about their need to avenge family harm, and he wondered whether there were any other members of the Lutz clan liable to continue the reprisals. Bodie thought about the matter, but he didn't let it worry him.

By the time he reached Hayes it was already dark. Bodie rode in along the rutted street, between the rows of lamplit buildings, and reined in beside the town jail. The main door was open, left in that position by some hopeful individual waiting for a cooling breeze.

The man sitting behind the cluttered desk in the small, stifling office glanced up at Bodie's tall figure. He stared at Bodie for long seconds and then a wide smile creased his square, brown face.

"Bodie! Hell, boy, it's good to see you!" He stood up, coming round the desk to take Bodie's outstretched hand in a powerful grip. "Last I heard you was up in the Nations. Mind that was six months back. You catch anything?"

"Little money and a little lead," Bodie remarked, thinking of the puckered scar running across his left side. "Anyhow, what're you doing wearing a badge for a ten cent town like this, Will?"

"You know what they say, Bodie. It's a living." Will Cross motioned Bodie to sit down. "I know one thing. It won't take more'n one try guessin' what brought you here."

"Hoyt Reefer," Bodie admitted.

Cross sighed, leaning his hip against the side of the desk. "Bodie, when you going to quit all this goddam chasing about an' put on a badge again?"

"Never, Will," Bodie snapped angrily. "No chance!" His voice still revealed the bitterness he felt, a bitterness that had made him what he was, changing him and his way of life. There were few men alive who would dare to confront Bodie with that episode from his past and expect to get away with it. Will

Cross was one of those few. Though even he knew he was wasting his time. He knew it every time he met Bodie and brought up the subject. Yet he also knew that he would keep trying. But for now he let it pass.

"Can't tell you much about Reefer," he said abruptly. He moved round the desk to a map of the territory which was pinned to the wall. Poked a finger at it. "I trailed 'em into the foothills," he said, tracing the route with his finger. "Lost 'em somewhere hereabouts. Hell, you know what the Guadalupes are like. Damn near all rock in that area. Needed a better man than me. Somebody like you, Bodie."

"Flattery will get you everywhere," Bodie grinned. "Make a guess, Will. Where do you think they were heading?"

"Hoyt Reefer plus stolen guns? That part of the country?" Cross gazed at the map again, then jabbed at the paper.

"Llano Estacado!" Bodie said. "I figure the same. Gun running to the Commanch'."

"Son of a bitch!" Cross exclaimed. "I hope you catch him, Bodie. And when you do, put in a couple of shots for me!"

"If there's room," Bodie promised. He stood up, easing the stiffness of his long ride from his body. "Will, is there a good place to eat in this damn town of yours?"

Cross snatched up his hat. "Yeah. Come on and I'll buy you a steak that'll make your mouth water like a dry creek after a flash flood!"

Cross was as good as his word. The small restaurant served the best food Bodie had eaten in a long time. Later they moved on to a small saloon where they shared a bottle and a few memories. They talked until ten o'clock and then Cross had to leave to do his tour of the town.

"Hey, will I see you in the morning?" he asked.

Bodie shrugged. "Maybe. I'll be leaving early."

Cross hesitated, reluctant to go, and

slightly embarrassed at the moment of parting. "Be seeing you, Bodie," he said gruffly and left the saloon.

For a time Bodie toyed with his drink, a sudden restlessness coming over him. It was, he knew, the rememberance of the old days, the sudden flood of long-cold memories brought to light. Many of them were dark, painful memories, which he would have preferred to have lain dormant.

He became aware of curious eyes on him. He glanced up and looked into the face of a young and beautiful Mexican girl. She smiled at him, her full, soft red lips parting moistly, exposing her small white teeth. As she moved slightly, her long hair, black and shiny, caught the light from the lamps hanging from the ceiling.

"*Buenos noches*, Senor," she murmured. Her voice was soft, with a gentle, husky inviting tone.

"Join me?" Bodie asked on impulse. There were worse ways to spend a lonely evening.

"Si!" The girl took the chair Cross had vacated. She leaned forward against the table, still smiling in that friendly, inviting way. Under the thin white blouse her taut, rounded breasts moved freely, jutting nipples darkening the sheer cloth. "I saw you with the marshal. You talked like old friends."

"A good friend," Bodie said. "From way back."

"*Bueno!*" The girl tossed her head to move hair away from her face. "To have friends is to be alive! I like to have many friends, hombre! I would like very much to be your friend. My name is Lita."

Bodie looked at her and thought, why not? He had nothing else to do. Already there was a familiar stirring in his loins, a reminder that his life had been pretty bleak of late, and Bodie had the same rule for women as he had for food and rest: take it when you can, when circumstances allow, because you might have to go a damn long time without it one day. "All right, Lita, you

74

lead the way. I feel I'm getting an urge to be real friendly."

Lita proved to be extremely friendly. In her small, one roomed adobe hut at the far end of town, she entertained Bodie in the most friendly act of all. Her lithe, brown, velvet-smooth body, with its curves and hollows, full-blossomed breasts tipped by dark, hard nipples, contrived to entrap Bodie in a tangle of naked flesh. She drew him between her long, lovely thighs, down to her tender moistness concealed beneath the triangle of soft black hair, letting him thrust his aching hardness deep into her eager flesh. As she lay beneath him on the tangled sheets of her bed, moaning in her pleasure, Bodie strove to meet her increasing demand for further satisfaction, and it was with a silent prayer of thanks that he finally drifted off into sleep, still locked in Lita's warm embrace and breathing in the musky fragrance of her flesh.

5

LYING on his belly in the coarse grass sprouting along the dusty ridge, Bodie studied the layout of the Comanche camp below. It had taken him five long, uncomfortable days to find the place. Picking up the long cold trail left by Hoyt Reefer and his gang, then losing it, wasting time while he rode back and forth across the rocky foothills of the bleak Guadalupes. Finally he had located a steady run of tracks, mainly left by the wagon the gang were still using to transport the stolen guns. The trail had curved off east, then gradually north. Up into the endless, silent Llano Estacado — The Staked Plains — the ancestral home of the Comanche. A vast and empty wilderness. Here the Comanches felt safe. It was their land. They knew it better than any white men, and they used that advantage to the full. Bodie always felt slightly uneasy riding this country. He liked to know where he was going and to have at least a small knowledge of his surroundings. The Llano was like some alien land. It was as hostile as the Comanche. It was not advisable for white men to venture alone into the Llano. To be honest it was not advisable for white men in groups to venture into the Llano.

Bodie stirred restlessly. Sweat soaked the back of his shirt. The sun was slowly, but surely, broiling him. The back of his neck stung from the relentless heat and there was a heavy pulsing inside his skull. He stared down at the encampment and wondered just what the hell he expected to gain from watching the place. He knew damn well that Hoyt Reefer and his gang were long gone. All he had to do now was to find out which way they'd gone when they left. Bodie sighed, reaching for his canteen. He took a slow swallow of warm water. Goddam heat! Got to everything! He felt grimy runnels trickle down his face. He sleeved the dampness away with the back of his hand, aware of the thick stubble irritating his skin. Jesus Christ, he thought, I'd give every cent of Trask's 10,000 dollars for a hot bath, a shave and a change of clothes, if I could have them right this minute!

He turned his attention back to the Comanche encampment. It was small. No more than half a dozen hide-lodges standing in the shade of leafy cottonwoods straggling along the edge of a shallow creek. A makeshift brush and pole corral had been erected to hold the Comanche ponies. Bodie could see a couple of cookfires sending thin spirals of smoke skywards. He had counted around a dozen Comanches in and around the camp. There were no women or children, so he figured that it was the camp of a raiding party.

Bodie was about to shift his gaze to the far end of the camp when he spotted movement at the entrance to one of the lodges. He saw two figures emerge, pausing to shield their eyes from the sudden glare of the sun. Bodie took a longer look and swore forcibly.

The two men, standing talking now, were not Comanches. They wore white mens' clothing! Had guns strapped around their waists. Bodie wished he was closer to the camp. He wanted to see the faces of the two men. Were they Reefer's men? He decided they must be. Were there more in camp? He would have to find out. It was the only way. He had to be sure who the men were. If they weren't from Reefer's gang he wanted to know so he wasn't forced to waste any more time. That meant getting closer to the camp. Much closer . . .

The soft whisper of sound almost escaped him. But a tiny fragment caught his ear, drawing his attention. Bodie's eyes flickered to the ground just to one side and forward of him. He saw the dark shadow thrown by the man now behind him. A shadow which grew, seeming to rise and envelope him.

Bodie twisted over onto his back, dragging his Colt from the holster, eyes seeking the attacker. He had a quick glimpse of a savagely scowling face. Black, greasy hair drifted across his face. Bodie absorbed a swift impression of a half-naked Comanche lunging at him, knife in hand. Bodie didn't have time to fire. He simply lashed at the face with the barrel of his gun. He felt the barrel connect with a meaty crack. The Comanche grunted as the hard metal split the flesh of his face wide open. The white gleam of exposed cheekbone showed for a second before a rush of blood welled up from the torn flesh. The Comanche made a wild swing with the knife, but it was inches away from Bodie. Pain had affected the Comanche's accuracy. While the Comanche's body was slightly twisted away from him, Bodie swung the Colt again. He clubbed the Indian along the side of his head, then struck again as the Comanche jerked back in pain. The barrel of the Colt smashed brutally across the Comanche's nose. Bone splintered and the nose flattened. Blood gushed out in bright streams. Bodie lashed out with the toe of his boot, burying it deeply in the Indian's groin. The Comanche let out an agonised howl, crumbling away from Bodie, giving him the moments he needed to climb to his feet. He wished he could use the Colt on the Comanche but daren't risk the sound of a shot carrying to the other Indians in the camp below. As the Comanche straightened up, thrusting his knife out before him, Bodie lunged forward. His left hand caught the Comanche's knife wrist, forcing it up. Bodie's right, still holding the heavy Colt, slashed down at the Comanche's unprotected face. Blood sprayed up in bright beads as the glinting barrel did its deadly work. Flesh tore, pulped, bone cracking under the stunning impact. The Comanche flopped to his knees, moaning softly.

The knife slipped easily from his fingers and into Bodie's hand. Bodie put away his Colt. Without hesitation he took hold of the Comanche's black hair and yanked the Indian's head back. For a moment the Comanche's eyes stared into Bodie's and from the ruined, bloody mask of his face. Then Bodie made a single, savage cut with the keen-bladed knife, laying open the Comanche's throat from ear to ear. A gaping wound opened in the taut throat. Severed flesh, muscle, arteries were exposed, and then blood spurted heavily from the wound. The Comanche jerked in silent reaction to the shock of pain, flopping over onto the blood-dappled ground.

Bodie went to his horse. He knew that he was at risk here. The last thing he needed was a Comanche raiding party on his trail, especially now that he'd gone and killed one of them.

He was about to mount when there was a soft hiss of sound. Something ripped cruelly across the muscle of his left arm, drawing blood. Bodie glanced up. Only yards away was another Comanche. This one carried a bow and he was in the act of notching a second arrow. Bodie knew that he wasn't going to outrun any arrows. There was no place to go. His only way to avoid being impaled lay in the holster on his right hip. Bodie realised what would happen if he used his gun. But he also knew what would take place if he didn't stop the Comanche with the bow. And there was no time to consider the matter.

Bodie thrust himself away from the horse, hitting the ground on his shoulder, rolling and coming up firing. His first bullet took the Comanche in the left shoulder, and burst clear in a pulpy spray of flesh and blood. His next shot hit the Comanche in the chest, snapping the upper ribs before ploughing on to tear the heart apart. The Comanche went over backwards, arms and legs thrown stiffly apart in shock.

Making a grab for the dangling reins Bodie hauled himself into the saddle, yanking the horse's head round and ramming his heels in. The animal gathered itself and made a run for the low hills a distance away. Bodie forgot about Reefer's men. He forgot about the $20,000 bounty. Right at that moment nothing mattered except putting some distance between himself and the Comanche camp just below the ridge. Bodie knew that when two dead Indians were found his life wouldn't be worth a wooden cent if the Comanches got their hands on him. He had seen victims of Comanche torture and they were sights that stayed with a man for a long time. They were things that nightmares were made of. Bodie had no wish to become one of those nightmares.

He rode hard and fast, knowing that he needed the distance, yet also aware that he was doing the one most fatal thing a man could do out here. He was pushing his horse to the limit.

The rugged terrain, the constant, brutal heat, the lack of water. All were reasons why he shouldn't ride his horse the way he was. The spur to urge him on, though, was too strong to resist.

Bodie put his horse up the lower slopes of the hills. He could feel it begin to labour as the slope became steeper. He risked a halt, dragging the horse round so that he could check his backtrail.

And felt a hard jolt of fear in his gut.

Far below him, but moving steadily towards the hills, were four Comanches on wiry ponies. Bodie watched them for a moment. Then, a silent decision made, he dismounted and pulled his Winchester from the saddle-scabbard. He edged along the slope until he found a wedge of flaking rock rising out of the earth. Settling behind it Bodie used the top of the rock as a rest. He levered a round into the chamber and sighted over one-hundred-and-fifty yards. Well within the range of the

Winchester. Bodie had owned the rifle for a good few years and he had it shooting as true as any weapon around. He eased back on the trigger while he aimed, holding back on the final fraction of trigger-pull. For long seconds he held his target in the sights, lifting as the bullet sped from the barrel. Bodie jerked another bullet into the chamber. Below, his target jerked suddenly in the savage aftermath of a .44 calibre rifle bullet ripping through his stomach, then slid from the back of his pony.

The other Comanches reined in their ponies. They began to argue amongst themselves as to what to do next. In the scant seconds that passed Bodie fired another shot and put down a second Comanche. This one flopped to the ground, screaming in pure agony, his right eye blasted away by Bodie's bullet, the ruined socket streaming blood.

The remaining Comanches turned their ponies away. One decided he couldn't leave behind his wounded comrade and rode back to help. Bodie let him reach the wounded Indian, then shot him off the back of his pony with a bullet through the head. The Comanche rolled back off his pony, hitting the ground on the back of his neck. Bone snapped and the Comanche's head sagged to an odd angle.

One Comanche remained. He made no attempt to return. He kept riding until he was well out of range, then reined in and sat waiting for more Indians to join him.

That was how Bodie left the place. With three Comanches down, one standing watch, and more than likely the rest of the raiding party coming to join the fight. Bodie didn't stop to find out. He climbed back into the saddle and rode on.

Dry grass rattled under the hooves of Bodie's horse as he took it across a flat meadow, edged with tall trees. At the far side a shallow creek glinted in the sunlight. The water looked cool and inviting but Bodie rejected the invitation to stop. He put his horse through the water at a dead run. Silver spray rose, soaking horse and rider. Then he was across, thundering up the grassy rise of the ground, into the shadow-dappled gloom of the trees. Hoofbeats were muffled by the carpet of leaves for the time Bodie drove his horse through the trees. Abruptly he was clear, the hammer-beat of the sun striking him with stunning force. He leaned forward across the horse's lathered neck, coaxing it on, well aware that his life depended on the animal's stamina.

He rode north for a time then began to swing east. Something at the back of his mind, maybe the animal instinct he often depended upon, told him it was the way to go. Overriding his survival instinct, demanding attention, his mind could not fully ignore the purpose for which he had come out here to the Llano Estacado. Hoyt Reefer and his gang! And that instinct determined his line of travel. If he was wrong he would try again. Circle and pick up tracks. But if he was right, and if he managed to shake off the pursuit of the Comanches, then he would once again take up his trail. Bodie had built up a deadly reputation as a hunter of men. There were no half-measures in his profession. Bodie was the best. It was not affectation. Simply an awareness of his capabilities. It earned him the respect of some, the envy of others, and the hatred of many. It had even earned him a title, often used when men spoke of him. Never in his presence. But Bodie had come to hear of it, and though he never acknowledged it, the title remained. When men came together to talk and the subject turned to bounty hunting there was always one name at the forefront of their conversation.

That of Bodie!

The hunter of men who didn't understand the meaning of the word failure. The man who, it was said, would trail a man clear to hell and fight the Devil himself for the bounty!

Bodie — the man they called The Stalker!

6

DURING the shadowed hours of the night Bodie lost the pursuing Comanches.

He maintained a strong lead throughout the day, and as the sun went down he had drifted into a wide, barren stretch of volcanic rock. The lava beds, a frequent sight in the parched badlands, were sterile relics of a long-ago period when the earth had been young. Thrown up during the violent upheavals of the earth's formation, they remained as mute reminders of creation: black, lifeless masses of fissured rock. Formed into twisted mazes, tunnelled and crevassed, scoured by the dusty winds, seared by the brutal sun. Changed and ripped asunder by physical and climatic changes that had taken place thousands of years ago . . .

Bodie had led his weary horse into the lava. Stumbling, cursing his own weariness, eyes aching from the day-long glare of the sun, he had drawn his horse deeper into the lava, seeking some remote place where he could rest.

In his haste to get away from the Comanche camp Bodie had left his canteen behind. Now he was parched. Mouth dry. Throat aching from reflexive swallowing. He longed for a taste of cool water. But the longing only made the lack of water harder to bear. Without thought he brushed the back of his hand across his mouth, wincing at the pulse of pain from cracked, dry lips. He tasted the salty tang of blood on the top of his tongue.

Easing his way down a ridged slope Bodie found himself in a dim, cavernlike place. He moved in deeper, aware of a pleasant coolness in the air. Pausing he listened, picking up the distant echo of trickling water.

He moved on, going further into the cavern. The undulating ceiling was no more than four feet above him. The light was fading fast when he rounded a bend and saw before him a shaft of pale light coming down a natural chimney of rock. The light illuminated the shimmering water in a wide, deep basin. The source was some spring deep in the rock. Bodie could see the silver bubbles rising to the surface of the pool.

Dropping the reins and letting his horse fend for itself, Bodie bellied down and took a mouthful of water. It was icy cold and was the sweetest water he'd ever tasted. He drank sparingly, well aware of the penalties for swallowing too much water after a forced deprivation. Bodie pulled off his hat and tossed it to one side. Leaning right over the pool he plunged his head in, rinsing the gritty dust from his face. He sat up shedding water like a dog. Brushing back his thick dark hair Bodie picked up his hat, knocking the dust free before he jammed it back on. Climbing to his feet he went to where his horse stood, its head down in the water. He took a little of the food remaining in his saddle bags, threw his blanket roll down, and ate.

As the light coming down through the rock gradually faded, Bodie unsaddled his horse and secured it. Then he rolled up in his blankets and settled down for the night. He kept his handgun with him beneath the blanket. His rifle was propped up against the rock close by. He was certain he had lost the Comanches, but it didn't cost him a thing to stay careful. He went to sleep knowing that his horse would warn him if he had visitors.

He saw no one. Bodie might have been the last man alive during the next two days. After leaving behind the lava beds he had made wide sweeps back and forth across the empty land, looking for signs. During the afternoon of the first day he picked up day old tracks. They had been made by two horses. It seemed he might have been right about the two white men he'd spotted back in the Comanche camp. He followed the tracks and they led him to a small ranch nestling in well-watered land close to the Brazos.

It was a lonely place, miles from anywhere, owned and run by three brothers named Brock. Or it had been. Now there were only two of the brothers still living. The third lay in a fresh grave. Bodie rode in to face a shotgun welcome and realised he was going to have to tread carefully until he had convinced the men holding the deadly weapons that he meant them no harm.

"You keep both your hands in sight, mister!" Clem Brock snapped, moving to one side of Bodie's horse while his elder brother, Henry, walked slowly round to the other side.

"Convince me you shouldn't get both barrels through your belly an' maybe I'll ease off this trigger," Henry suggested. His broad face bore the livid marks of a recent beating. One eye was almost shut, the pupil barely showing. The flesh around it was swollen, purple and yellow. His lips were split and puffy.

"I'm looking for two men," Bodie said. "Seems you might have found 'em first."

Clem eyes him warily. "You the law or somethin'?" he asked.

"Or somethin'," Bodie told him.

The elder one cleared his throat and spat. "Goddam bounty hunter! You want to bet me I'm wrong, Clem?" He inched the shotgun closer to Bodie. "Maybe I still should blow you out the saddle!"

"What's eating you, friend?" Bodie asked.

"Far as I'm concerned you ain't no better than those two bastards who killed Will," Henry Brock yelled. "Bunch of animals is all!"

"Easy now, Henry," Clem Brock said. He lowered his shotgun. "Look, mister, I were you, I'd move on. We

96

don't need any trouble. I figure we had enough the last couple of days. You'll have to excuse Henry. Those two . . . well they roughed him up pretty bad. Then when they shot down Will . . . it hit Henry awful bad."

"I'm just after them," Bodie said. "I'm not looking for anything else."

"Then get the hell off our land, mister," Henry yelled. He gestured violently with the shotgun, his face darkening with anger. "Go peddle your goddamn business some other place!"

Without another word Henry Brock turned and stalked off towards the low, adobe and timber cabin.

"Just answer me one question," Bodie asked.

"What?"

"Those men. You hear any names?"

Clem Brock nodded. "I recall hearing one call the other Largo. That's all I can tell you." He glanced towards the fresh grave. "Now ride out, mister, 'fore Henry works himself up to bein' in a shootin' mood!"

"What were they after?" Bodie asked gently, not prodding because Clem Brock wasn't in the mood to be pushed.

Clem Brock started to lift his shotgun then changed his mind. He lowered the weapon, shoulders sagging. "What the hell! You want to know what those bastards killed for? I'll tell you, mister. Two goddam horses is all! They'd ridden their mounts to a standstill an' wanted fresh ones. When we didn't agree they pulled guns on us. One of 'em beat up on Henry, an' when Will got mad enough to try somethin' the one called Largo just shot him down!"

"Figures," Bodie said.

"Sounds like you know 'em well."

"I know 'em. Those two belong to Hoyt Reefer's bunch. I trailed 'em from a Comanche camp where they been selling guns."

A wild look showed in Clem Brock's eyes. "Bastards! I wish I could get my hands on the sons of bitches!" He stared hard at Bodie. "It true what Henry said? About you bein' a bounty hunter?"

"Yeah."

"You aim to bring those bastards in alive?"

Bodie smiled mirthlessly. "Far as I'm concerned they're dead already," he said.

Clem Brock nodded in satisfaction. "When you kill 'em, mister," he said, "make 'em feel every shot!"

Bodie reined about and moved off across the yard, away from the ranch, picking up the trail left by Reefer's two men.

Mid morning of the following day he came in sight of his quarry. To be precise he sighted the place where they had temporarily gone to ground. It was no more than a sprawling old trading post, stuck down in the middle of nowhere. A long, low adobe building. A couple of smaller huts. Off to one side stood a rickety corral, the fence posts bleached white, dried out and split.

Dotted about the place were various oddments from dismantled wagons, empty barrels, half-rotted boxes. At one end of the main building was a stack of empty bottles. A pile of rotting food was black with wildly buzzing flies. A faintly sweet smell, that of decay, hung over the place. As Bodie rode in he spotted a couple of mangy dogs lurking in shaded corners. A few scrawny chickens paraded across the hard-packed dusty yard. Passing the corral he looked over the horses and spotted two wearing brands on their hips in the form of a large letter B inside a circle. It was the same brand he'd seen on cattle near the Brock ranch.

There was a sagging hitch rail outside the main building. Bodie eased out of the saddle, looping his reins over the rail. Glancing over the top of his saddle he saw a door in one of the smaller huts swing open. A naked Mexican woman appeared. She leaned casually against the doorframe, watching Bodie. There was an expression of utter boredom on her brown face. Tangled black hair hung thickly across her shoulders. As Bodie emerged from behind his horse the woman stretched, yawning, large, well-shaped breasts quivering with her movements. Then she reached down and lazily scratched at her matt of black pubic hair. Her gaze met Bodie's and she stared at him defiantly.

Smiling to himself Bodie reached the door and pushed it open. He stepped into a room that ran the length of the building and took up a great part of its width. A press of stale air reached Bodie's nostrils as he took a quick glance about him. The room was an untidy mess. A conglomeration of store and saloon. Goods were stacked haphazardly in every available foot of space, piled on shelves, even hung from the ceiling. Further along the room a bar had been built from thick planks placed on the top of large barrels. Shelves behind the bar held bottles and glasses. A couple of tables and a number of chairs stood in a clear section of floor.

Bodie made his way down the bar. He had already spotted the figure behind the counter. A huge, bald-headed man, who was watching Bodie's approach with open hostility. He leaned against the edge of the bar, arms braced against the scarred top, his great hands spread flat.

"You want somethin'?" the man asked, his tone indicating that Bodie's answer ought to be in the negative.

Bodie glanced about him, taking note of the doorway at the far end of the bar. He turned his attention to the surly bartender.

"Could be," Bodie said.

The bartender's face twitched with agitation. "Then make up your mind, bucko, 'cause I ain't standin' here waitin' for the daisies to grow!"

"The two fellers who rode in on the Circle-B horses. They still here?"

The bartender's reaction was immediate — and violent. His left hand swept up from the bar, powerful fingers fastening on Bodie's shirt. Yanking the manhunter towards him the bartender wrapped his other arm round Bodie's neck, hugging him tightly to his barrel chest. Bodie felt his throat constrict, precious air being cut off.

"Hey, Eddie! In here! We got trouble!" The bartender's voice bellowed his alarm with enough force to rattle the bottles on the shelf behind him.

Bodie, half-dragged across the bar, struggled to maintain some kind of balance. He was at a distinct disadvantage but by no means helpless. He realised he wasn't going to break the grip of the powerful arm about his neck, which was expected of him. So he used all his strength to swing his body all the way across the bar. He caught the bartender unaware. The big man went backwards, smashing into the bottle-stacked shelves behind him. Bottles splintered, spilling liquor. The bartender gasped as keen slivers of shattered glass drove into the flesh of his lower back. The sudden pain caused his grip to loosen slightly, giving Bodie a chance to gulp in quick breaths of air. The moment his feet touched the floor Bodie made a grab for his holstered Colt, but the bartender's free hand slapped the gun from Bodie's fingers as it came from the holster. At the same time he regained his crippling hold around Bodie's neck, throwing his other arm around Bodie's body. Bodie felt his ribs move under the pressure, and he knew that if he didn't do something fast he was going to be crushed. He kicked out against the edge of the bar behind him, getting enough force to shove the bartender up against the shelves again. More bottles were dislodged, smashing as they hit the floor. Bodie threw out a hand, fingers searching blindly. He slid his hand along a shelf, felt the sharp bite of broken glass. Ignoring the pain he thrust his hand against the shelf again. He touched the cold shape of a bottle and closed his fingers over the neck. The bartender became aware of what he was doing and lunged away from the shelves. He rammed Bodie's body up against the edge of the bar, bending him back, against the natural curve of the spine. Cold sweat broke out on Bodie's face as pain flared up in protest. He gripped the bottle tight in his fingers and struck it against the hard edge of the bar. The bottle bounced off the hard wood. Bodie struck a second time. The bottle broke, splintered glass exploding across the bar.

The bartender, perhaps only just realising his own vulnerability raised his voice in a final yell for help

"Eddie!"

Bodie brought up his right hand, holding the shattered bottle. There was a soft, moist ripping sound as the jagged edges of the broken glass sank into the bartender's neck, just beneath the jawline. Bodie gave the bottle a half turn as it sank in, gouging a raw, deep wound. The bartender uttered a loud, terrified scream that turned into a whimpering gurgle as blood welled up from the wound, then became a spurting stream as the jagged glass sliced through the main artery. Bodie felt the hot flood soak his shirt. He jammed a hand beneath the bartender's chin and forced the dying man's head back. Even then it took long seconds before the bartender slackened his grip enough for Bodie to pull free.

Gasping for breath Bodie stumbled along the edge of the bar. He saw the bartender, his shirt drenched in scarlet, flop to his knees, rolling over onto his back like some huge beached whale. He lay on the floor amongst the broken glass and spilt liquor, his blood spattering everything around him.

Bodie spotted his Colt and picked it up. As he straightened he heard a soft footstep close by. Twisting his head he looked into the face of a man who could have been the bartender's double if it hadn't been for the thinner features, the thinning brown hair. The man had come through the door at the other end of the bar. He had already seen the bloody figure on the floor, and he continued his forward motion, closing rapidly on Bodie. There was no time for avoiding a confrontation. No way that Bodie was going to stop this man except one. He had seen the upraised double-edged axe the man held in his hands. The axe was already on the downswing of a stroke intended to split open Bodie's skull if he didn't get out of the way. The big room reverberated to the blast of Bodie's Colt. He fired three shots, knowing that he had to put this man down fast and for good. His bullets ripped bloody debris from the man's body. The impact of the heavy .45 calibres spun the man off to one side. He slammed up against the wall, bouncing off to smash up against the edge of the bar before he pitched face down on the floor in a spreading pool of his own blood. The gleaming axe slid from his fingers, slicing through the air no more than a half inch from Bodie's face, before it thudded into the wall where it hung, quivering.

Bodie stood upright, thumbing fresh loads into his Colt. He took a passing glance at the axe as he stepped by and touched a finger to his unshaven cheek.

"Close shaves are one thing," he said dryly, "but that was damned ridiculous!"

He stepped round the bar and headed for the door. Something told him to get back outside quickly. He was still heading for the door when he heard the unmistakable whinney of a horse. Then another. He ran, throwing open the door, going straight outside.

Two men were at the corral. One had the gate open and was trying to catch one of the agitated horses. Dust rose in grey clouds from beneath nervous hooves. The second man was dragging a pair of saddles towards the open corral. They were close enough for Bodie to be able to recognise them. They were the men he had seen at the

Comanche camp. He could put names to them now. One was Jesse Largo, the man Clem Brock had identified. The other was Lee Kendal. Both of them members of Hoyt Reefer's gang.

"Hold it, boys, you ain't going anywhere," Bodie yelled.

Largo stopped chasing horses, spinning with enviable speed, his gun appearing in his hand almost without motion. He fired once, then changed position, firing again. But Bodie had already altered his stance, dropping to a crouch, his own colt up and firing. His first shot was for Lee Kendal. It caught the man as he was still trying to draw his own weapon. The bullet blasted a hole right through Kendal's lean body, emerging in a pulped gush of blood and flesh. Kendal stumbled back against the corral gate, his arms becoming entangled in the cross-posts, and he hung there like some abandoned scarecrow. Even while his first bullet was finding its target Bodie had hit the ground, pushing his Colt out before him, seeking Largo's shifting figure. The man was no fool, Bodie realised. He had the sense to keep moving, changing his position and his stance, so that he presented a continually changing target. But this time he was up against an opponent who practised the same technique. It put Largo slightly off his stride. He allowed himself to hesitate for an instant. To try and locate his target long enough to hold a steady aim. Bodie used the moment for the same reason. He didn't take anywhere near as long as Largo when it came to aiming. His Colt moved only fractionally before he fired. Jesse Largo went down on one knee as Brodie's bullet took the top of his left shoulder off in a burst of red. Bodie's next shot was exactly placed. Largo's head went back with a snap as a .45 calibre bullet ripped into his skull directly between his eyes. Blood squirted in a bright red stream from the entry wound. Largo flopped over on his back, limbs jerking in a senseless rhythm.

Bodie walked over to where Largo lay in pooling blood. He kicked aside Largo's gun, then moved on to check Lee Kendal. Putting a boot against Kendal's body Bodie gave a none too gentle shove. Kendal's lifeless corpse flopped away from the corral gate and sprawled face down in the dirt.

A shadow fell across the ground near Largo's head. Bodie glanced up and saw the Mexican woman he'd noticed earlier. She had put on a thin cotton dress now, though it did little to conceal the ripe curves of her lush body. Up close Bodie could see that she was much younger than he had first thought. She peered at Largo, then across at Kendal. Her brown face puckered into a frown of annoyance.

"Muerto?" she asked.

"If they're not somebody's putting on a damn good act," Bodie said.

The Mexican woman muttered under her breath. "All that time they were here," she said angrily, "and they never paid me!" She lashed out with a bare

111

foot at Largo's body. "Bastardo! Only an Americano would get himself shot just to avoid paying for his pleasure!"

"It's a hard life," Bodie sympathised.

The Mexican woman turned her attention to the tall American, eyeing him with a view to business. She watched the easy way he moved. The supple strength of the body under the dusty, bloodstreaked clothing. Now here, she thought, was a man she would gladly perform for free of charge.

"Hey, hombre," she whispered huskily. "You maybe have the time to keep me company for a while?"

Bodie glanced at her. The thin dress clung to her sturdy body, outlining the heavy shape of her breasts. It followed the slight swell of her stomach, then moulded itself to the ripe thighs, and the soft fullness between.

"Honey," he said, "I've heard of stepping into a dead man's shoes, but you've just gone and given the saying a whole new meaning!"

7

HE came trailing down out of the shimmering Texas wasteland, a dust-grimed, silent figure astride a weary horse. A pair of rope-led horses followed in his wake, each carrying a blanket-wrapped shape. A hovering cloud of black flies hung over each motionless load. It just happened to be a Sunday morning and the town's stonebuilt church was letting out the congregation as the rider came in along San Rico's main street. The single bell in the church tower was pealing, sending its message across the rooftops of the small town.

As he rode by the church, ignoring the hostile stares of San Rico's citizens, Bodie glanced up at the church tower. He could see the bell swinging back and forth. A smile touched the corners of his taut mouth.

113

"Hear that, boys," he said softly, directing his words in the direction of the two corpses he was leading, "they're playing your tune."

Reaching the town's central Plaza Bodie cut off across the square, reining in at the hitch rail in front of the jail. He eased his stiff body out of the saddle, tied his horse and went into the jail. The office was cool compared to the day's sullen heat. Bodie took off his hat, knocking dust from his shirt as he crossed the stone-flagged floor.

The man seated behind the desk in the far corner of the office glanced up at Bodie's entrance. He was a florid, overweight man with small, feral eyes. Thin, greased-down hair with a centre parting, hung over his protruding ears. He stared at Bodie coldly, pursing his thick, wet lips.

"You the marshal?" Bodie asked.

The man pushed aside the magazine he'd been studying and leaned back in his creaking swivel chair. A scratched badge was pinned to the front of his creased shirt. He let the badge answer Bodie's question, and continued to stare at his visitor.

The man's attitude got under Bodie's skin. He'd ridden for two days from the trading post to San Rico. The trip had been long and dirty and he'd been plagued by clouds of filthy, buzzing flies attracted by the sickly-sweet odour of dead flesh. Largo and Kendal might have been silent companions, but they had made their presence felt in another way. Now he was in San Rico all Bodie wanted was a chance to send a message to Lyle Trask, telling him he could pick up two of Reefer's boys. After that Bodie wanted a bath, a meal, a day in bed, and a change of clothing — in that order. When he'd satisfied his physical needs he would take up the trail of Hoyt Reefer and the remaining members of the gang. The Mexican woman back at the trading post had been one of the talkative kind. She had told Bodie all about the things that had gone on at the post, which had turned out to be a refuge for anyone on the wrong side of the law. The pair who had run the place — the ones who had tried to kill Bodie . . . the Ruskin brothers, had been a law unto themselves. The post had been a meeting place for outlaws. A place where stolen goods were bought and sold. Where information flowed as freely as the whisky. As far as the Mexican woman had been concerned Bodie had done the world a good turn in killing the Ruskins. Before Bodie had left he'd watched the woman help herself to money from the dead men's strongbox. Then she had filled a sack with supplies, saddled a good horse from the corral and freed all the others. Her final act before riding off had been to set fire to the trading post. Then she had ridden back towards the border, to the small village where she had originally come from over six years back, before raiding Comanches had slaughtered most of the villagers, carrying her off and used her to satisfy themselves during the ride up through Texas. Eventually she had been sold off to the Ruskins who had kept her as an added attraction for their frequent guests. During the course of her conversation with Bodie she had managed to give him one solid lead to the whereabouts of Hoyt Reefer and his gang. During their stay at the post, Largo and Kendal had referred to a man named Jim Kelly. He worked, it seemed, in a saloon in Anderson's Halt, a small community that had sprung up around what had initially been nothing more than a way-station for one of the cross country stagelines. Anderson's had suddenly blossomed when the Union Pacific railroad had decided to run a line through that part of the country, making the way-station a permanent stop. It meant more business for the stageline, turning an ordinary stop into a bustling connecting point for travellers. The new importance attracted others with an eye for the easy dollar. Almost before the first train stopped at Anderson's there had sprung up a restaurant, a couple of saloons, a hotel, even a brothel. Anderson's Halt, once a quiet speck of civilisation on the banks of the San Saba, burst into noisy life, and was never the same again. Jim Kelly was one of the newcomers to Anderson's. He was a gambler working for a percentage in a saloon some wit had named The Traveller's Choice. The only choice a traveller might have was whether to actually go into the place. Once he was through the door choice was the last thing he was allowed. It was to this saloon and to the man named Kelly that Hoyt Reefer was heading. Kelly, it seemed, had information to sell which he knew Reefer would buy. Largo and Kendal were to have joined Reefer at a later date, at an unspecified location. That didn't worry Bodie. His interest was centered around Jim Kelly. If Bodie could learn the information Kelly had passed to Reefer then he would be able to ride directly to where Reefer was located. All that was ahead of Bodie. First he had to settle the matter of Largo and Kendal. He wanted to be rid of them. He was tired and dirty and hungry — and the manner in which the marshal of San Rico was treating him did little to soothe Bodie's short-fused mood.

"Got a couple of dead ones outside," he said flatly. Bodie unfolded the 'Wanted' posters for Largo and Kendal, dropping them in front of the marshal. "Jesse Largo. Lee Kendal. Couple of Hoyt Reefer's boys. Like you to identify them, marshal, then clear up the paperwork so I can collect my money. Three thousand between them. It's on the sheets."

"I can read," the marshal grunted. He snatched up the posters and stared at them. "Outside are they?" he asked in a voice which indicated he thought it was a lot of trouble having to even go and take a look.

"I could drag 'em inside for you," Bodie offered sarcastically. "Be a bit of a stink but we'd manage."

The marshal hauled himself upright. When he stood his large stomach sagged and flopped over his gunbelt. He picked up a spotless cream stetson and jammed it on his head, then led the way outside. An irate group of men were gathered near the two horses. As the marshal appeared they moved towards him. A thin-faced man in his early fifties, dressed in a pearl grey suit broke free from the crowd and wagged a finger at the marshal.

"This is outrageous, Pritt! These foul-smelling corpses being paraded through town for women and children to see!"

Marshal Pritt took a breath of the decay issuing from the dead outlaws and backed off. He coughed a couple of times to clear his throat.

"I ain't about to go and take a close look at those two, mister," he said to Bodie. "You'll have to wait until they can be dealt with."

Bodie's face hardened. He grabbed

hold of the marshal's fat arm, his fingers gripping with the power of a steel trap.

"You listen to me, mister! I ain't about to wait. Now you can either sign those papers after you've looked or before you've looked or nothing but trouble is going to come your way!"

Pritt stared at him through wide eyes. This man frightened him and Pritt wasn't about to argue with him right at this particular moment in time.

"I can sort it out for you," Pritt scowled. "Give me an hour or so."

The man in the pearl grey suit ran his gaze over Bodie, making his disapproval obvious. "I don't know who you are, sir, but we can do without your sort in San Rico. I suggest you leave at the earliest opportunity."

Bodie turned his back on the man and walked away.

"You hear what I say?" the man yelled.

Bodie turned and stared at the man. "The way you're shouting, feller, I reckon the whole damn town can hear you. If I was you I'd quieten down. Don't you know it's Sunday?"

The man's face darkened. He took a step forward, seeming ready to continue with the words he was having with the tall stranger. But something made him check his anger. He abruptly turned about and walked off.

Bodie smiled to himself and carried on up the street. He spotted a young Mexican boy sitting on the edge of the boardwalk and beckoned him over.

"See the horse at the hitch rail outside the jail? I want you to take him to the best livery stable in town. Tell the man I want the horse rubbed down, fed and watered. The best of everything he's got. You tell him if he doesn't look after the horse I'll want his hide!"

The boy grinned from ear to ear. "Si, senor, I will tell him."

Bodie pulled out three silver dollars and gave them to the boy. "Those are for you, chico. Be some more if you look after the horse."

"Gracias, senor!" The boy turned and ran down the street to where Bodie's horse was waiting.

Bodie made his way across the town until he reached San Rico's small rail depot. He went inside the small telegraph office and sent a message to Lyle Trask, telling him of Largo and Kendal's deaths. He didn't say anything about the lead he had to Hoyt Reefer. The message ended with instructions for Trask to send someone to collect the corpses. From the depot Bodie went to the town undertaker. The owner wasn't too keen to open on Sunday, but Bodie's insistence overcame the man's objections. Bodie told the man to collect the bodies from the marshal, do what he could to preserve them, and put them in a couple of cheap coffins to wait for Trask's pickup. With his business over Bodie went looking for a meal. He finally found what he was looking for and sat down to ham and eggs, fried potatoes and fresh baked bread. He worked his way through a full pot of coffee too. The meal over, he went looking for the barbershop.

He was making his way up towards the Plaza, where the barbershop was situated, and was just passing an alley when strong hands reached out, caught hold of his shirt and dragged him into the alley. Bodie had a quick glimpse of hard, brutal faces leering at him, then he was forcibly rammed up against a hard brick wall. Something clubbed brutally across the side of his skull, driving him to his knees. A red mist obscured his vision. Before he could stand up the toe of a boot smashed across his ribs. Bodie's breath burst from his body in a ragged grunt of agony. Hands caught hold of him, hauled him to his feet. Bodie caught a blurred glimpse of a man stepping in front of him. Off to one side a man giggled. Then a hard fist came out of nowhere and drove against his mouth. Bodie's lips split, blood streaking his face. His head rocked back from the blow.

"Hold the son of a bitch still!" a man's voice rasped out of the mist.

"Easy for you to talk, Redigo," a second voice whined. "You ain't got to hold the big bastard on his feet!"

"Don't fret, Banjo, you'll get your bloody turn. Right now he's mine!"

The final word was emphasised by a vicious blow to Bodie's taut stomach. White hot shafts of pain exploded. Bodie went up on his toes, part out of agony, part out of a realisation that if he didn't start fighting back these unknown attackers were going to beat him senseless. As he stretched Bodie felt the man behind him lose his grip slightly. Coming down onto the soles of his feet again Bodie let his knees bend, then thrust up and back, putting everything he had into the sudden move. He heard the man behind him yell a warning. Then the man was smashed hard against the side of the building on that side of the alley. Bodie felt the hands on him drop away. He twisted round, swinging both arms up, fists clenched together, clubbing the winded man full in the face. There was a sound of breaking bone and the man's face was suddenly wet with blood, his jaw sagging loose.

The moment he'd hit the man Bodie dropped to a crouch, turning his face the second of his attackers, the one he'd heard called Redigo. He caught a glimpse of a hulking shape, a tall, big-built man with a gaunt angry face. Redigo came at Bodie in a rush, arms flailing wildly. Bodie let him come close then stepped aside, easily avoiding Redigo's bull-like charge. As Redigo lumbered by Bodie drove his right foot up into the man's groin. Redigo let out an agonised bellow. Before he could control his forward motion he smashed bodily into the building. Following him, Bodie took hold of his shirt, yanking him away from the building. Redigo gave a wild curse and swung a huge fist. Bodie batted it aside, then punched Redigo in the face. Redigo's thick lips were pulped, blood spurting. He coughed, spitting blood and broken teeth. He was still spitting when Bodie hit him again and again and kept hitting him until Redigo was a moaning, bloody wreck crawling round the alley on his hands and knees.

Bodie took out his Colt and went to where the other man, Banjo, slumped awkwardly against the wall of the building. He had both hands cupped against his bleeding face. Banjo stumbled back as he saw Bodie approaching. He stood very still when he saw the gun in Bodie's hand.

"All right, you bastard, talk to me," Bodie snapped. He put his left hand flat against Banjo's chest, pinning the man against the wall at his back, then placed the muzzle of his Colt against Banjo's cheek. "Why?"

Banjo's eyes rolled in their sockets. He shook his head, mumbling through his bloody fingers.

Bodie eased the Colt's hammer back. He saw thick beads of sweat form on

Banjo's face. "You better start giving me the answers I need, feller," he said. "Don't be fooled. I'll kill you as soon as look at you!"

Banjo stared into Bodie's angry face, looking beyond the bloody features, and found himself eye to eye with Death.

"Back off, mister," he begged. He lowered his hands from his broken jaw. He could only speak slowly, with great difficulty and pain. "It was . . . Cremont . . . Ashley Cremont. He wanted — you worked over — bad."

"Who the hell is Cremont?"

"The feller . . . you . . . had words with on the street."

"In the grey suit?"

Banjo nodded. "Cremont walks . . . tall in San Rico, mister. You don't talk back to Ashley Cremont."

"How much did he pay you?" Bodie demanded.

Banjo groaned as pain flared in his jaw. "Hundred dollars each to rough you up and ride you out of town."

"Give it me," Bodie said.

Banjo fumbled a roll of banknotes from his shirt pocket and handed it to Bodie. "What you going to do with it?"

Bodie put away his gun. He smiled at Banjo. A wolf's smile. Cold and merciless. "I'm going to give the man his money back. Got to be fair. You boys didn't earn it."

He turned and left the alley. Crossing the Plaza he went into the jail. Marshal Pritt glanced up from his desk. He stared at Bodie's bloody face.

"What the hell happened to you?"

Bodie waved the crumpled roll of notes under Pritt's fat nose. "That happened! Two bastards jumped me. Names of Banjo and Redigo. They were supposed to beat the shit out of me and get me out of town."

Pritt's face paled. "Who in hell would . . . ?" His voice trailed off and he stared hard at Bodie, his face colouring rapidly.

"Cremont!" Bodie said softly, making

no attempt to conceal the menace in his tone.

"You expecting me to do something about it?"

Bodie shook his head. "No chance, Pritt! This is all mine!"

Pritt came halfway up out of his chair as Bodie made for the door. "For God's sake, just take it easy. Cremont ain't some forty-a-month cowhand! The man owns most of San Rico!"

Bodie paused at the door. "Then he ought to hire better people to do his dirty work. Where will I find him, Pritt?"

The marshal sighed in defeat. "Over the street. He's got an office in back of the store. After church on Sundays he takes his missus home then spends a few hours working. I tell you, though, he won't like being disturbed. Nobody ever goes near him on Sunday when he's working."

"Well he's going to have his routine changed today."

Pritt grabbed a paper off his desk.

130

"Hey! I never did get round to askin' your name. I need it for the paperwork on these bounty claims."

"Just put Bodie!"

Marshal Pritt stared after the tall man as he crossed the street. He got up and peered through the dusty office window. Jesus H. Christ! If only he'd known! He would have kept his mouth shut. There he'd been near enough arguing with the deadliest manhunter of them all. The man with a reputation so high he had most of the so-called gunfighters look like old ladies. And now he was here in San Rico. About to walk in on Ashley Cremont and bust his ass! Pritt had no love for Cremont. The man was a damned nuisance. Throwing his weight about all the damn time. Well he wouldn't get much change from Bodie. Not the man they called The Stalker!

Bodie wasn't aware that Marshal Pritt was watching him as he crossed the street. Not that it made any difference. Ashley Cremont was the only matter to concern him at that moment. The man's name was painted in big bold letters over the front of the store. The glass-paned double doors were locked. Bodie put his shoulder against the junction of the two doors and shoved. He felt the doors open inwards a little, then hold against the lock. Bodie gave another, harder shove. Something splintered and the doors swung open. Bodie went inside, closing the doors behind him. He crossed the shadowed floor of the store, making his way behind the counter and through the door at the rear. He found himself in a narrow passage. A number of doors led off to various sections of the rear area. At the far end of the passage was a final door. There was a small wooden plaque on the door with gold-painted letters which read: Ashley Cremont — Private Office — No Admission. Bodie reached for the doorknob, then paused, listening.

Whatever work Ashley Cremont indulged himself in on Sunday mornings it seemed that the services of a female were required. The sounds coming from behind the closed door indicated that the work was most likely to be of the physical kind. Bodie put his hand out and turned the doorknob. The door was locked. Stepping back Bodie put his shoulder to the door, the force of his blow snapping the lock and sending the door flying open.

The girl standing in the centre of the office carpet couldn't have been more than eighteen years old. Her naked body still held the ripe freshness of youth. Creamy white flesh, firm and smooth. Soft dark hair tumbling in thick curls to the upper slopes of her high, ample young breasts. Rosy-pink nipples jutting erect and soft, silky hair nestling at the junction of her long, shapely thighs. As the door crashed open she jerked her head towards the sound. Apart from that she exhibited no reaction to Bodie's sudden appearance.

Ashley Cremont, however, gave a

more positive response. He threw Bodie a wild-eyed look and began to get up off his knees. Cremont was kneeling in front of the girl, naked himself except for a pair of calf-length grey socks held up by suspenders. His thin, pale body looked almost skeletal against the girl's healthy development. Jerking to his feet Cremont uttered a startled cry and lunged for his clothing draped on a nearby chair. Bodie blocked his way. Red faced, Cremont made a grab for his clothes. Bodie slapped him across the face with the back of his hand. Cremont stumbled away. He suddenly became aware of his exposed manhood, thrusting stiffly erect, and he made a vain attempt to cover himself.

"God, man, what kind of animal are you?" Cremont blustered.

"Wasn't me on my knees sniffing the daisies," Bodie reminded him, glancing at the girl. She had retreated to the big desk standing in one corner of the room and had leaned her firm buttocks against the edge. Her eyes caught Bodie's and she smiled at him as if to say, I don't give a damn!

"Just what do you want?" Cremont demanded, though his tone lost a lot of power due to his nakedness.

Bodie held up the crumpled money he'd taken from Banjo. "For a businessman, Cremont, you make lousy decisions. Next time you want somebody beaten up pick men who can do the job. I've brought your money back. Those tramps didn't earn it!"

"I don't know what you mean," Cremont insisted.

"The hell you don't," Bodie said, losing all patience. He punched Cremont in the mouth. Cremont went flying back, blood gushing from his pulped lips. He stumbled and fell, then began to crawl away from Bodie's advancing figure, whimpering softly. Bodie reached down and hauled Cremont to his feet. He spun the man round to face him, then hit him again. The force of the blow spun Cremont across the room. He banged up against the wall, clawing at the wood panels. His legs gave and he slumped to the floor where he lay in a lewd, sprawled out position. Bodie crumpled up the money in his fist and dropped it on Cremont's blood streaked body.

"Hey, what about me?" the girl asked.

Bodie glanced at her and smiled. "Honey, if I had the time you wouldn't need to ask that question. I was you I'd get the hell out of here, cause when that son of a bitch wakes up he ain't going to be in the best mood."

The girl crossed the room and began to get dressed. "I think you're right, mister," she said. "He isn't all that cheerful when he's happy. You know what I mean?"

"I sure do honey," Bodie said, and left. He had an appointment at the barbershop and he didn't want to get there and find the damn place closed, it being Sunday and all.

8

ANDERSON'S HALT was an unlovely collection of buildings squatting on the north bank of the San Seba. The river ran west to east across the Edward's Plateau and the grubby little town, with little that could be called appealing, deposited its rubbish in the muddy waters of the meandering stream. From the original way station Anderson's Halt had mushroomed into a hybrid town. A hotch-potch collection of structures, each built where its particular owner or company decided was best for his or its interests. There had been little planning during the new construction, so that the main street of Anderson's Halt was a crooked, dusty ribbon winding its way through the buildings.

Riding in, late in the evening, Bodie noticed with weary eyes that there was at least a telegraph office. He pushed his horse on down the street. It may have been late, but Anderson's Halt was far from being ready to retire. A train was standing in the depot, muted lamplight showing behind blind-covered carriage windows. The locomotive belched clouds of smoke from its stack and white clouds of steam from hissing valves. A small knot of passengers moved from the train, across the street and into the semi-comfort of the Transit House, a hotel run by the railroad and the stageline. Riding on by the depot Bodie moved along the street. Here and there he saw businesses still open for custom: a couple of restaurants, gambling parlours and, of course, the saloons. They blazed with light and hummed with activity, and none more than the Traveller's Choice. It was the largest and the most garish of the lot. Light spilled from every window. So did noise. There was a constant roar of men talking, shouting, laughing, arguing, and shrill sounds coming from female throats. Somewhere, almost lost beneath the roar, Bodie could hear a piano.

Bodie was almost deafened as he stepped inside. He threaded his way through the crowd, making his way to the bar where he ordered a beer. He was surprised to find it cold. In most saloons beer was usually flat and lukewarm. As he drank Bodie scanned the saloon. It didn't take him long to locate what he was looking for. At the far end of the big room a section had been partitioned off. On the other side of the partition were the gambling tables. Every table was busy, too, Bodie saw.

A girl, dressed in a flimsy, scarlet dress, cut low at the front to reveal most of her full white breast, caught Bodie's eye and came over. She was about twenty-five, with curly red hair and eyes that had seen a lot for her age. She stood, one hand on her curved hip, surveying Bodie as if she was sizing up a champion bull.

"Ain't seen you round here before, big boy," she said. Her voice was soft, with a pleasing drawl to it.

"That's cause I ain't been here before," Bodie told her. "Now, you wouldn't be in the mood for a drink, would you?"

The girl laughed. "I declare you read my mind!"

Bodie beckoned the closest bartender over. "Drink for the lady," he said. "Hey, don't charge me two dollars for a glass of coloured lemonade. Give her a real drink."

"Thanks, big boy, I could do with one. Jesus, I've been on my feet so damn long, my behind don't remember what sitting is any more."

Bodie waited until her drink arrived. He picked up his own glass and motioned for the girl to follow him. Bodie stopped at a table where two grizzled cowhands were stolidly sitting over empty glasses.

"The boys here won't mind movin' on now they've finished their drinks.

Not when there's a lady waiting to sit down. Will you, boys?"

"Go to hell, mister, and take the tail with you!" one of the cowhands said.

Bodie leaned over and spoke softly in the man's ear. When he straightened up the cowhand stared at him, his face paling a little. After a few seconds he stood up, still glaring at Bodie. His partner rose, too. For a few seconds the two parties stared at each other. Then the cowhands turned and pushed their way out of the saloon.

Bodie placed the drinks on the table and they both sat down. Facing the girl Bodie watched her drink.

"Hey, what did you say to those cowboys to make 'em move to fast?" she asked.

A smile flickered across Bodie's face for an instant. But he didn't say a word. The girl dismissed the question from her mind and concentrated on her drink.

"You don't know how good it is to be sitting down," she began a minute later. "You want anything tonight you just ask for it."

"If you feel like trading all I want is information," Bodie told her.

The girl shrugged. "And I thought you were going to be fun."

"The night ain't over yet," Bodie smiled.

"I'll keep you to that," the girl said. "Now what's all this about information?"

"You've got a feller working here on the tables. Name of Jim Kelly."

The girl nodded. "Yeah! Old quick fingers himself! Mister, it just isn't safe to get near that creep. He's the kind who sees a girl in a skirt and just has to put his hand up it!"

"Point him out for me," Bodie said. "But don't make a thing of it."

The girl frowned, wondering if she ought to get involved. She decided there was no reason why she shouldn't.

"See the first table? There's a big man in a grey suit. Bald head. On his right is a skinny feller in black.

142

Shirt with a lacy front. Black hair all greased down. Little moustache. That's Kelly. Makes me shudder just looking at him. I don't know what it is but he upsets me. Maybe I don't like his wandering hands. Or his wandering eyes. You'd think I'd be used to it working in this game. But not with him. Not in a hundred years."

"Not one of your favourite people?" Bodie took a good look at the man named Kelly. Just another gambler. A fancy dresser who most probably imagined himself a real ladies' man. Kelly had a sharp, almost sly face. There and then, Bodie decided that Jim Kelly was not a man to trust.

"You got business with Kelly?" the girl inquired, studying Bodie across the rim of her glass.

"A little," Bodie answered. "Won't take long."

The girl smiled at that. She leaned forward a little. "I'm kind of pleased about that."

"What time does he quit for the night."

"Kelly? Oh, usually around midnight. He's no late night bird. Got a room at the hotel just up the street."

"Thanks," Bodie said. "You want another drink?"

The girl tapped her empty glass on the table. "Guess so. This one seems to have sprung a leak." She grinned suddenly at him. "Hey, big boy, you trying to get me drunk or something?"

"Never know your luck."

"What do they call you, big boy?"

"Bodie."

"Well, Bodie, I finish around midnight, too. And they call me Sherry."

They shared a second drink and then Sherry reluctantly went back to her job. Bodie watched her move from table to table, coaxing the customers to buy drinks. Laughing with them, flirting, teasing. He could see she was a popular girl. There was enough of her genuine personality coming through to conceal the cold facts of her ultimate aim. To get the customers to spend their money. On drink. Or on gambling. Or on one of the girls who might be willing to provide more than just casual chatter.

The evening wore on and Bodie took time to find somewhere he could get a meal. He ate sparingly and was back in the saloon by half past eleven. The place was still crowded, seemingly more noisy than it had been earlier. Jim Kelly was still seated at his table, hunched over his cards, a long, thin cigar dangling from his pale lips. Bodie glanced across the noisy saloon, looking for Sherry. He finally spotted her as she linked arms with a bearded old man who appeared to be in the act of buying drinks for the entire saloon.

The big clock on the wall above the main bar crept around to twelve. Then ten past. Jim Kelly carried on playing. Sighing Bodie ordered another drink and settled himself in his seat. The gambler carried on for another ten minutes before the game was completed.

At the same time that Kelly got up from behind his table and moved towards the saloon door, Sherry, a thin cape thrown across her shoulders appeared at Bodie's table.

"Seems as if everybody's working late tonight," she said.

"You finished now?" Bodie asked, his eyes on Kelly's slow moving figure.

"Yes. If you still want I'll be over the street in the restaurant having coffee. I mean, after you've settled your business with Kelly."

"I'll be back," Bodie said and stood up.

He shouldered his way through the crowd and out onto the boardwalk. Glancing along the shadowed verandah he spotted Kelly. The gambler was strolling along, taking his time. Probably taking in a lungful of fresh air after the long hours in the smoky saloon. Bodie fell in behind the gambler, keeping his distance. He didn't want to tackle the man until they were reasonably alone.

Moving away from the saloon Bodie noticed that this part of town was pretty quiet. All the businesses were closed, lamps extinguished. The street was shadowed, deserted, almost menacing.

The faint scrape of a boot on worn planking warned Bodie too late. He whirled in towards the sound, sensing the sudden presence of a lurking shape. His hand darted for the butt of his Colt, but his fingertips had barely touched the smooth wood when a solid shape smashed down across the side of his head. The blow stunned him, the night opening up in a white-hot cascade of blinding light. Numbing pain filled Bodie's skull. His legs refused to obey his mental commands and he pitched face down on the boardwalk, rolling over the edge onto the dirty street.

He lay in a foggy daze, only partly aware of the sounds around him. He fought to gain control of his leaden limbs. He tried to focus his senses. Dimly he heard the sound of running feet. Then a yell, like a man shouting down a well, the sound hollow, unreal. Then a silence. Followed by another yell. This time a recognisable sound.

Someone in fear!

Abruptly the misty world around Bodie was blasted apart by the heavy boom of a gun. A second blast followed the first. Mingled with the sounds came yet another yell, quickly rising to a high, awful scream of terrible agony!

Then silence. Broken after a few minutes by a low, shuddering moan. A broken, animal like sound. It was a sound Bodie could recognise, even in his dazed state. It was the sound of a fatally wounded man suffering in overwhelming pain. It was a sound Bodie had heard many times in his life. Perhaps too many times for his own good!

It was the last sound he heard for some time. Everything slipped away. He fell forward into an abyss, a deep, dank, lonely pit of utter darkness.

9

"**B**ODIE, it's a good thing you've got a hard head."

Bodie didn't bother to speak but he agreed with Sherry's observation. The clout on the skull had left him with a pulsing headache and a three-inch gash. Apart from that he was slowly beginning to feel human again. Sherry's ministrations were helping his recovery no end. She'd had him brought to her room, over one of the stores, and had tended to his wound personally. Bodie had slept through the night and with the rising of the sun had woken to the aroma of freshly brewed coffee, and the sight of Sherry moving about the small room completely naked. On hearing him stir she had filled a china mug with coffee, sweetened it and brought it to him.

"Somebody must have it in for you,

Bodie," she said.

Bodie tasted the coffee, letting the strong brew flow down his throat and warm his insides. "Me and Jim Kelly," he said.

Sherry shuddered at the memory. The movement caused her breasts to quiver, half-erect nipples puckering. "It was horrible. I've never seen a man killed before. He didn't even look human. They said it must have been a shotgun. Both barrels fired up close."

Why hadn't they killed him? The question kept thrusting itself forward in his mind. He answered logically. Maybe because they only wanted Jim Kelly. Gamblers often made enemies. Men who had lost money. Maybe more. Bad losers. There were any number of reasons why Jim Kelly might have been killed. But the thought still nagged. Even if Kelly had been the target Bodie could have been a witness. If Bodie had been in the killer's place he wouldn't have left behind a man who might possibly be able to point a finger.

"You want some more coffee?" Sherry asked. Bodie handed her the mug and watched her cross the room, hips swaying gently, buttocks jutting firm and round. "Anything else I can get you?" she asked over her shoulder.

Like excited? Bodie thought as he watched her. He glanced down at the other half of the big bed, noticing the rumpled sheet. A wry grin touched his lips. Damnation, he thought. There he'd gone and spent the night in bed with her and all he'd done was sleep! He felt himself hardening at the thought. He became aware, too, that he was naked.

"You have help last night?" he asked as Sherry brought his refilled mug to the bedside. She placed it on the small table close by and stood frowning down at him, hands on her supple hips. "Getting my boots off and all, I mean!"

Sherry smiled, a mocking twinkle in her eyes. "What makes you think I need any help in getting a man undressed?" She sat down on the edge of the bed and leaned in towards him, the rising tips of her breasts brushing his chest. "In fact it was fun, Bodie. You know what I mean?"

"Appears to me the fun's all been going one way," Bodie remarked.

"Then how about getting it to change direction?" Sherry murmured huskily. She reached out and drew the blankets from his body. A warm sigh escaped from her soft lips when she saw his risen hardness and she laid a warm hand across it, fingers curling to grasp him with surprising tenderness. Bodie drew her to him, closing his mouth over hers. Sherry slid the length of her body onto his, thighs spreading, easing her hand clear so that she could feel his hardness through the soft crown of curly pubic hair. She twisted her hips, moaning softly as rising sensations coursed through her. She submitted willingly when Bodie turned her onto her back, pushing her warm thighs wider apart with his own. He entered her easily, feeling the heated moistness close over his erection, then he was fully inside her. Sherry closed her thighs about him, straining hungrily, her lithe body squirming, thrusting, arching up off the bed as she responded to him. And there was no sound except their harsh breathing and the soft creak of the bedsprings, until the moment when they climaxed, and Sherry threw back her head, a long, satisfied moan rising in her taut white throat, then silence. A long, drawn out, fulfilled silence . . .

Later, still naked, she lay and watched him dress stretched out across the bed in a deliberately provocative pose, hoping that she might get him to stay.

"There any kind of law in this place?" Bodie asked.

Sherry pouted, then scowled, finally sat up, brushing stray curls of red hair back from her face. "No," she said.

"They keep talking about hiring a marshal. Until they do we got to depend on the US Marshal. He comes by once in a while."

Bodie strapped on his gun. He slid the Colt out of the holster and checked the loads. Satisfied, he put the gun away, picked up his hat.

"Bodie, am I going to see you again?"

He opened the door, glanced over his shoulder. "Sherry, there ain't no way I can answer that. I leave here — I don't know where I'll end up."

She slid off the bed and crossed to kiss him, lingering, taut nipples brushing his arm. "Hey, Bodie, it was good, wasn't it?"

"Sure," he said. "Trouble is it don't seem so important once it's over. It's like pain. While you got it you figure nothing could ever be as bad, but once it's over, no matter how bad, then you get to thinking and wondering why you made all the damn fuss at the time."

Sherry stared at him, anger gleaming in her eyes. "Goddamn it, Bodie, you are one son of a bitch!"

"So I been told," Bodie tugged on his hat. "I get the chance maybe I'll call in before I ride on."

"Don't do me any favours, Bodie," she snapped, but her eyes were saying something entirely different.

Out on the street Bodie made his way to the livery stable where his horse had been housed for the night. Satisfying himself that the animal was being cared for he retraced his steps back along the street. His destination was the hotel Jim Kelly had been using. Kelly was dead and there was no way Bodie could get information he'd had for Hoyt Reefer. But there was a possibility, however slight, that there might be something down on paper. It was worth taking the time to visit Kelly's room.

The hotel was a miserable place. Raw, unpainted lumber, scant furnishings. It had been built to serve a basic need.

Somewhere for people to sleep. For Jim Kelly it would have been entirely suitable. A place where he could lie down and rest between long sessions at the poker tables. Kelly wouldn't have wanted more. He was a transient, a drifter, moving from one location to the next. There was no kind of permanency in the lives of men like Kelly. It seemed to be part of their make-up. All gamblers were saddled with a need for change, for fresh pastures. Maybe it was something to do with their need for challenge, the urge that drove them to gamble in the first place.

Bodie crossed the gloomy lobby of the hotel and watched the desk clerk drag himself wearily from his seat behind the desk.

"Hey, you're the feller who got clouted last night when Jim Kelly got hisself shot up!" the clerk gobbled. He was a tall, skinny young man with round, bulging eyes. "Boy, was he blown to hell and back! You see him? I did! Up real close too! I ain't never seen a feller done with a shotgun 'fore. Handguns and rifles, yeah. I even seen a guy cut open with a knife once. That was over in Fort Worth. Had his belly slit wide open. Jesus, you could see what he'd had for breakfast!"

"What do you do when you're on holiday?" Bodie asked quietly. "Buy ringside seats for hangings?"

The clerk closed his loose mouth and stared at Bodie's grim face. He attempted a weak smile, though it came out like a ghastly leer. "I didn't mean . . . anything . . . Mister Bodie . . . it was . . . !"

"Keep your hobby to yourself, boy, and give me the key to Kelly's room."

The clerk's eyes bulged even more. "Hell, I can't do that. I got to keep that room locked until the US Marshal gets here. Them was his orders over the telegraph."

"When does he get here?" Bodie asked.

"Day after tomorrow," the clerk answered triumphantly, figuring he'd scored over Bodie.

"Then he'll be too late to stop me," Bodie said. He thrust out a big, menacing hand. "Now give me that key, boy, or you're in for a real treat. You'll be able to feel what it's like having *your* belly sliced open!"

The clerk's pasty face turned fish-belly white. He gave a strangle moan and lunged for the board behind him where all the room keys were kept on hooks. Taking one down he handed it to Bodie.

"The Marshal, he's going to be mad as all hell!"

Bodie, on the first step of the stairs, shrugged. "Tell him I said I was real sorry!"

Reaching the top of the stairs Bodie walked along the passage until he reached room 8, the number on the key-tag in his hand. He unlocked the thin, warped door and shoved it open. Inside he closed and locked it from his side. He didn't want anyone walking in on him.

The room was small, stark, functional. No paint on the walls. No decorations at all. Just a bed against one wall. A clothes chest and a washstand. A chair beside the bed. Bodie went to the window and rolled up the blind. He slid open the window and let in some fresh air to wash away the lingering smell of sweat and urine.

He checked the clothes chest first. It revealed nothing except Jim Kelly's meagre wardrobe. A couple of white shirts. Underclothes, socks. A pile of white linen handkerchiefs. On the washstand were Kelly's razor and brush. A couple of bottles of scented hair lotion. On the floor beside the bed were a pair of black half-boots. On its side was a half-empty bottle of cheap whisky. Under the chair Bodie saw a ragged old carpetbag. He picked it up and carried it to the clothes chest, tipping the contents on its scarred top. Tossing the bag aside after checking to see it was empty, Bodie examined the scattered contents. A few odds and ends of dirty clothing. A bundle of long cigars. A few letters. Two from a woman in Baton Rouge, asking when he was going to come back to see her. The letters were months old. The woman had been waiting a long time. Now she was going to have the rest of her life to wait. The final letter Bodie picked up was no more than a few days old. He pulled the folded sheet of paper from the crumpled envelope and opened it. There was no sender's address on the paper. Nor was it directed at Kelly. It simply stated: 'shipment leaves Austin for Fort Worth, 24th this month.' That was all. Bodie reread the cryptic message again. A shipment? Of what? If Reefer was involved it was most likely to be guns. Assuming so, a shipment of guns was leaving Austin on the 24th and heading in the direction of Fort Worth. Bodie realised he was only guessing at the letter's meaning. He had no proof that the message was connected with Hoyt Reefer. Or that it implied anything mysterious. He glanced at the envelope, noticed something on the back and smiled to himself.

It was a small sketch-map, drawn crudely in pencil. A meandering line, with place-names along its length. Fort Worth at the top, Austin at the bottom, and Waco midway along. Between Austin and Waco another line, bisecting the main one, marked San Gabriel. Above this a small cross and the legend. 'Water halt. Tower 6'. Someone had ringed this in heavy black pencil. Bodie folded the envelope and put it in his pocket. The map had been childishly simple to decipher. It was a diagram of the Austin-Fort Worth railroad. San Gabriel meant the river. The ringed cross implied a chosen location. Bodie saw it as the place where Hoyt Reefer and his gang might conceivably make a strike at the train carrying the shipment mentioned in the letter. And the more he thought about it the more he became convinced that the shipment would turn out to be guns. Weapons ready to be stolen so that Reefer could supply his Comanche customers so they could go out and kill.

Bodie left the room and made his way back down to the lobby. He tossed the key to the scowling young clerk and stepped outside. He had little to go on. The letter and the map didn't spell out definitely what Reefer was up to. Instinct was pointing him in Reefer's direction. All Bodie could do was to follow his instinct and play whatever card fell into his hand.

He was on his way to the livery to pick up his horse and ride when he realised he was passing the store over which Sherry had her room. On an impulse he decided to call in and say goodbye. Turning into the alley beside the store he climbed the outside stairs and opened the door.

The room was silent except for the insistent buzzing of a couple of flies. Sunlight streamed in through the open window, throwing shafts of yellow across the bed. Sherry's naked body lay still on the crumpled sheet, arms and legs spread. Her head was turned in Bodie's direction, mouth open, eyes staring. But she didn't see him. Or hear him.

Sherry was dead.

Somebody had very skilfully cut her throat from ear to ear, laying open a huge gaping wound, severing the main arteries in the process. Bright gouts of blood had spurted freely, streaking Sherry's white flesh, running down her body and across her stomach, matting the curly triangle of pubic hair. Blood had spattered the white sheet she was lying on, spreading out all around her sprawled body and as Bodie moved closer he could see that beneath her the sheet was sodden, unable to absorb all of the blood that had poured from Sherry's body.

Bodie snatched out his Colt and moved quickly to the window. He knew, even as he did so, that he was wasting his time. Whoever had killed Sherry would be long gone now. He swore softly as he realised that the killer must have been waiting for him to leave. Then he had moved in quickly, killing silently, and then slipping away without even being noticed.

He made a swift check of the room and its contents. Nothing had been disturbed. It didn't look as if robbery had been the motive. What then? Bodie had a sneaking suspicion that Sherry's death was somehow linked with that of Jim Kelly the night before. The trouble was that the only connection between them was Bodie himself. He wondered if he was moving along the right track. Perhaps the deaths were the result of some argument. With some kind of deal that had gone wrong. Bodie reasoned that he could invent a hundred different reasons and still be wrong. Had Sherry's death anything to do with Kelly's involvement with Hoyt Reefer? Again he was only speculating. There was nothing else he could do until he could work out some logical explanation.

There had to be something behind it all. First Jim Kelly. And significantly just before Bodie had been able to get to him and find out what the man knew. Maybe that was the reason. Maybe Kelly had been in possession of too much information about Hoyt Reefer. Perhaps too much to be allowed to walk around with it. Again the reasoning didn't fit. Kelly's information had been invaluable to Reefer. So why would Reefer want him dead? There was always the chance that Reefer hadn't wanted Kelly dead, but someone else did.

Bodie slipped quietly out of Sherry's room. He made his way down the street, finding that there were few people about. He went to the livery stable, paid his bill and saddled up. Leading the horse up the street he stopped off at the first store and bought himself some extra supplies. As an afterthought he bought extra boxes of ammunition for his guns.

He rode out, and once clear of Anderson's Halt he cut off to the southeast, heading for the San Gabriel and an isolated water halt on the Austin-Fort Worth railroad.

10

BODIE picked up the gleaming twin tracks of the railroad on the morning of the second day out from Anderson's Halt. It was the 24th. He cut down out of dry hills and let his horse make its own pace. The sun had already curved its fiery way into the sweep of blue sky overhead and was hammering down on the desolate Texas landscape. A wind was beginning to drift through the brush, lifting gritty dust, rattling the brittle vegetation.

He had ridden hard from Anderson's Halt, stopping for only the briefest rest the night before. Now, as he neared the place he knew only as Tower 6, Bodie alerted himself. He drew his rifle from the scabbard and laid it across his thighs, one hand close to the lever. Somewhere up ahead of him, and not too far, was the tower where the train from Austin would stop to take on water. If Bodie's thinking was correct, there would be more than water waiting at Tower 6!

There would be a group of men who were ready and willing to kill to gain the shipment being transported to Fort Worth.

Time drifted by in a sultry haze. The wind increased, lifting more dust, sending writhing coils scudding across the sunbaked earth. Bodie rode with the minimum of effort, conserving his energy. Excessive movement in this climate was a sure and certain way to lose the body's natural moisture. A man could easily sweat himself dry. Dehydration could set in fast. Too many men had died through that kind of foolishness. Bodie had no intention of becoming one of them.

He saw the smoke first. Dark smudges against the blue sky. The wind caught it and tore it into ragged patches, lifting it high over the parched, empty land.

Bodie checked his horse, easing it away from the tracks. He took it through the thick brush and along a dry creekbed, keeping his eyes on the drifting smoke.

Then he heard the first shots. Sharp, urgent sounds rattling out from behind the thrusting rise of ground before him. He slid from the saddle, dragging his horse into the concealment of high brush. He tied the reins to a tough root, checked his rifle, and moved off in the direction of the shooting.

He crawled the last few yards, eyes narrowed against the drifting dust. On the crest of the rise he settled himself, and looked down on Tower 6.

There wasn't much to it. Just the high, trestled framework supporting the round wooden water tank. The long canvas flume hung on a weighted chain. That was Tower 6.

On the track beside the tower stood a motionless train. A steaming locomotive, black smoke rising from the sooty stack, coupled to a half dozen boxcars and a caboose.

The sliding doors of one boxcar were open. Bodie could see armed men clustered around the opening.

On the ground beside the caboose a still figure clad in the uniform of a railroad conductor lay in the twisted sprawl of death, blood staining the upturned back. A second man, in oily overalls, was slumped down beside the locomotive, hands clutched tightly over the bloody wound in his stomach.

Bodie watched the activity below with grim satisfaction. His guesswork had proved to be correct. He had already recognised Morgan Taylor and Jim Tyree, two of Reefer's men. There appeared to be at least six men down there, so it seemed that Reefer had hired a few extra guns to make up for the missing Largo and Kendal.

Even as Bodie watched he saw a tall, muscular figure step from the shadowed interior of the open boxcar and jump to the ground. Shaggy haired and unshaven, there was no concealing

170

the broad features of Hoyt Reefer, his face set in a hard scowl. The renegade gestured to his men and said something which Bodie couldn't catch.

A couple of Reefer's men climbed into the boxcar and began to slide long, narrow wooden cases to the open door. Bodie smiled. That was it! Cases of rifles. Probably there would also be boxes of ammunition. There were enough weapons down there to keep the Comanche and their Kiowa allies equipped for a long time. The knowledge angered Bodie. Out and out killers were bad enough. But Hoyt Reefer's brand of business had a foul stench clinging to it. There was something sick about a man who could trade in human lives the way Reefer did. Because that was what his dealing in guns meant. The guns were sold to the Indians who would use them on Reefer's own kind. Men, women and children would die at the hands of the Comanches. All through Hoyt Reefer's doing.

Bodie levered a round into the Winchester's breech and settled the rifle against his shoulder. It was time he went to work. Time he started to earn the bounty he'd ridden so far to collect. And killing Hoyt Reefer and his bunch would be a real pleasure!

The Winchester blasted flame, smoke whipping away from the muzzle as the wind caught it. Down below one of Reefer's men, bending to ease a case of rifles to the open door of the boxcar, was flung brutally against the thick frame of the door, his skull bursting apart in a shower of blood and bone and brains. As the lifeless corpse slumped to the floor of the boxcar a second shot came. Morgan Taylor, who had snatched his gun from his holster at the sound of the first shot, gave a shocked grunt as a bullet ripped through his left hip. Taylor went down in a welter of spurting blood, his drenched trousers also wet from urine from his relaxed bladder. He fell in a crumpled heap, falling back against one of the boxcar's wheels.

The moment he'd fired his second shot, Bodie got his feet beneath him and ran, crouching low, yards to the left. Reefer and his men were alerted and they would be spreading apart, finding cover, seeking the source of the shots. Dropping to the ground again Bodie peered over the rim, a grim smile etched across his face.

He watched as Hoyt Reefer and his men ran for cover. One of them was making for the slope from where Bodie was doing his shooting. Bodie let the man get a few yards up the slope before he shouldered the Winchester and drove three quick shots into the unprotected body. The man screamed once, a high sound that trailed off in a wet gurgle as rising blood burst from his mouth. He twisted to one side and tumbled back down the slope, kicking and twitching against the savage pain inflicted by Bodie's three bullets.

A gun opened up from below, bullets whacking into the slope just below the rim. Shortly, other guns joined in. Bodie rolled away from his position and moved along the rim in the other direction, thumbing fresh cartridges into the Winchester.

He heard a sudden rush of escaping steam from the stationary engine. As he flopped down in a fresh position he caught a quick glimpse of an overalled figure on the locomotive's footplate. The engineer, still alive, was making the most of the sudden distraction and was pulling out all the stops in an attempt to move his train. He succeeded too. The entire train gave a sudden lurch, couplings clanging noisily. The big driving wheels on the locomotive spun, showering bright sparks before traction was gained, and then the train rolled forward.

Morgan Taylor, barely conscious, felt the support at his back move. Through the fog of pain engulfing his body he experienced a jolt of fear. The train was moving! He was lying right up against the wheels too! Taylor made a vain attempt to roll clear. But the collar of his jacket had become hooked over one of the big nuts securing the wheel to the boxcar's axle. Taylor screamed once as the rotating wheel lifted him. Helpless, he was raised bodily. The top of his head smashed against the underside of the boxcar, splitting open his skull as if it was nothing more than a flimsy eggshell. Blood streamed down over Taylor's face. Still alive, Taylor flailed about in agony. As the wheel twisted him higher his collar ripped, freeing him. Taylor slumped to the ground and flopped back across the steel rail of the track. He had time for a fleeting awareness of where he was before the next set of wheels ran over him. The wheels spun his body over and over, leaving behind a long, grisly trail of pulped flesh, bone and greasy intrails.

Pulling back from the rim, which was exploding under the impact of repeated volleys of shots, Bodie made for a pile of eroded boulders. He was within yards of the rocks when he caught the drum of hooves. He realised he wasn't going to make the cover of the rocks and turned towards the rim of the slope.

Horse and rider burst into sight over the rim in a shower of dust and stones. Bodie had a blurred image of the rider, hatless, black hair streaming back from his wild-eyed face. The man's mouth was wide open in a yell of fury. He reined his horse round savagely, cutting in at Bodie, driving the horse forward. Bodie had no time to level his rifle. He saw the looming bulk of the horse leaping at him and thrust himself off to one side. Fast as he was Bodie felt the solid smash of the horse's hindquarters against his chest. The impact hurled him to the ground, his breath ripped from his lungs. He let himself roll, felt the Winchester torn from his grasp. Coughing and spitting dust from his mouth, Bodie dragged his feet under him, lunging upright, his right hand going for the Colt on his hip. He felt the familiar texture of the wood grips. Slid the heavy gun free, easing back the hammer as he half-turned, seeking the rider.

A gun blasted nearby. The bullet burned a bloody furrow across Bodie's left side. The man was struggling to settle his frisky horse and bring his own revolver to line up on Bodie.

Still in a crouch Bodie thrust his Colt forward, angling the muzzle up towards the rider's body. The rider yanked his own gun round in the same instant and the two men fired together. The shots merged into one heavy blast of sound.

Bodie threw himself forward the instant he'd pulled the trigger, landing on his left shoulder, rolling over twice, then throwing out his left hand to steady himself as he thrust the Colt out and up again, triggering two swift shots.

His first shot had taken two fingers from the rider's left hand, leaving behind a pair of mangled, bloody stumps. The final two bullets found their way into the mans' body just beneath the lower rib, tearing apart organs and muscles alike. One of them shattered the spinal cord just before it emerged from the base of the neck, a gush of mangled tissue gouting from the ragged wound. The rider fell back out of the saddle. He hit the ground on his face, but he was already beyond feeling any more pain.

Bodie climbed to his feet, running to where he's dropped his rifle. He snatched up the Winchester, continuing on towards the rim. A curse rose on his lips as he saw three horsemen spurring their mounts away from the railroad tracks. Bodie threw his rifle to his shoulder, aimed and fired.

The closest of the three riders threw up his arms and toppled from his saddle. He rolled over a few times, made a futile attempt to get to his feet, then fell face down on the ground and didn't move again.

The remaining pair of riders didn't

even look back. They simply spurred their horses on, finally vanishing beyond a long ridge.

Bodie checked the condition of the rider he'd taken out with the shot through the spine. The man was dead. He was not one of Reefer's regular men.

Making his way to where he's tethered his horse Bodie mounted up and rode down the slope. As he neared each body he checked to see whether they were alive. None were. There wasn't much left stretched along yards of steel rail. There was a lot of blood splashed around and big black flies were already hovering greedily over the pulped remains.

Dismounting, Bodie walked to where the last man he'd shot was lying. Bodie's bullet had gone in between the shoulders, splintering a rib on its way out. The man was lying on his stomach, blood soaking the ground beneath his body. He was still alive. Bodie turned him over and saw the gaping hole where the bullet had come out. With each breath the man took a bright flood of blood issued from the wound. Again the man was not one of Reefer's known men.

"Where're they headed?" Bodie asked when the man's eyes flickered open. "Reefer and Tyree, mister! I want to know!"

"Go . . . f—— yourself . . . !" the man hissed through tight clenched teeth. A long shudder racked his body. He stiffened abruptly, sweat gleaming across his gaunt face.

"I ain't got all day, you son of a bitch! Now tell me where they're heading!"

"How the hell . . . should . . . I . . . I . . . know!" The man's body spasmed violently. He coughed and bright blood flecked his lips. "Goddam you, mister . . . I ain't going to make it! I hope . . . you . . . rot in hell!"

"Won't we all," Bodie said and stood up. He knew that the man wasn't going to tell him anything. There was no point in wasting time.

"You goin' somewhere, mister?" the wounded man yelled.

Bodie paused and turned to look at the man. "Yeah. Why?"

"What about me? Shit, you son of a bitch, you can't just walk off and leave me like this! I need lookin' to! I need docterin!"

"I ain't no doctor," Bodie said.

The man yelled out suddenly as pain rose in his chest. He raised a pleading hand to Bodie. "For god's sake, mister, you got to give me something for this . . . this pain . . . please . . . please!"

"Sure," Bodie said easily. "I'll give you something and you won't ever feel a thing again!"

He lifted his Colt and put two bullets through the man's skull.

"Now see what you done," Bodie muttered as the dead man flopped back on the bloody earth. "All that fuss made you panic and lose your head!"

11

THE engineer had halted the train about a quarter mile down the track. Bodie rode out to meet him, persuading the man to bring the train back to the scene of the ambush. With the engineer's help Bodie loaded the dead bodies into one of the boxcars. In the caboose he found paper and wrote a note, addressing it to Lyle Trask.

"Is that *the* Lyle Trask?" the engineer asked.

Bodie nodded. "When you get to Fort Worth send a telegraph message to Trask and tell him to come and pick up the bodies."

The engineer frowned, scratching his head. "What is he? Some kind of weirdo? He goin' to have 'em stuffed or somthin'?"

"There's a thought," Bodie grinned.

"Just send the message I've written. Trask'll do the rest."

"Sure." The engineer watched Bodie check his horse. "You goin' after them two?"

Mounting up Bodie settled in his saddle. "Seems that way, feller."

The engineer climbed up to his cab. As he set his train in motion he glanced off towards the south. The rising wind had lifted a veil of yellow dust across the land, and the hard-riding man on the big horse had already been swallowed by the rolling mist.

The trail led due south. Reefer and Tyree were heading for the border. Bodie was certain of that. He became even more certain when the trail began to drift off towards the west. Reefer intended to lose himself in Mexico for a while. His gang had been shot to pieces, leaving him with a solitary survivor. Reefer would want time to think. Time to hire on new men before he took up his business again. Mexico could provide a sanctuary while he rested. It would also provide him with the men to rebuild his gang. There would be plenty of hungry guns ready to join up with Hoyt Reefer.

The hot wind tugged at Bodie's clothing, sifting dust into his eyes and nose. It filtered through his shirt, causing his skin to itch. It got into his mouth and left a sour, pasty taste to linger through the long daylight hours. Through it all Bodie kept riding, doggedly stalking his prey, and never once losing sight of the faint trail left by them in their hurried flight.

As darkness settled over the wide land Bodie found himself a place to camp. He tethered his horse and built himself a small fire. He didn't give a damn whether Reefer could see it or not. He hoped the renegade could. It would remind him that he hadn't been forgotten. That there was somebody on his backtrail. Following him. Sticking like glue.

Bodie fried himself a couple of thick slices of salt-bacon. He brewed up a pot of coffee. When he'd eaten his meal he cleared his gear away and sat back with a thin cigar. He could relax for a little time. Bodie made the most of it.

Beyond his small camp the limitless landscape lay bathed in faint moonlight. The dry wind was still moaning across the rolling miles of emptiness. Dust rattled against mesquite and catclaw.

Bodie's horse abruptly snorted, pulling back against its tether. The sound brought Bodie to his feet in a fluid movement, his Colt in his fist. He kicked dirt over his fire, plunging the campsite into darkness. Something other than the wind had startled the horse. What though? Man or animal. Bodie eased away from his horse and took a slow, careful walk around his camp. He saw nothing and heard nothing. Even so he spent a good half hour searching. Finally satisfied he returned to his blanket beside the extinguished fire.

If anyone, or anything had been

outside his camp, there was no sign of an intruder now. Bodie knew enough to be certain that he was alone again. But something had been out there. He felt a slight, but growing irritation. Something was going on that he knew nothing about. And Bodie did not like that. He hated mysteries. Especially when they involved him. He was thinking now about the strange deaths of Jim Kelly and the girl called Sherry back in Anderson's Halt. The odd way they had died still bothered Bodie. He'd been too involved up until now to give much thought to the murders. Now, though, with this mystery visitor, the subject thrust itself to the forefront of Bodie's mind.

Who had killed Jim Kelly? And Sherry? Why had they been killed? What was the connection between the two? Had it been because they both knew Hoyt Reefer? Bodie doubted that Reefer had been behind the killings. The renegade would have lost a good contact if he'd had Kelly blown apart.

And anyway, Reefer had been long gone when Kelly died. And what about Sherry? As far as Bodie had seen, Sherry was nothing more than a saloon-dixie who liked men. He smiled grimly to himself in the darkness. Liking men had got more than one girl killed. In Sherry's case he didn't think that was the reason. There was more to it.

Bodie tossed the problem back and forth in his mind, trying to find reasons. To answer questions he kept asking himself. He got nowhere. All he did get was tired. He drew his blanket round him and settled back. He slept lightly, his Colt in his hand under the blanket.

He woke in the chill dawn. Packing away his gear Bodie took a mouthful of water from his canteen before mounting up and riding on.

He cut the trail again after twenty minutes. After an hour's riding he came across the spot where Reefer and Tyree had camped the night. In the trampled earth around the blackened ring of the fire he found countless cigar butts. And lying on its side in the dirt was an empty tequila bottle.

Close on midday Bodie splashed across the muddy Colorado river, south of Austin, and found that the trail was still moving south and west. Ahead lay a vast, empty tract of arid terrain. A hostile land of searing sun and long waterless stretches. The next town of any size was San Antonio. Reefer might possibly stop off there. He could be in need of supplies. There was always the chance of picking up a couple of gunhands.

The sun was slipping out of sight off to the west when Bodie sighted the small ranch squatting on the banks of a clear-running creek. It was a sorry outfit. No more than a primitive adobe hut and a split-pole corral. There were probably a few dozen head of rangy longhorns running wild over the sparse range surrounding the place. Bodie rode in with a cautious reluctance, his rifle in his hand. He didn't like the silence. The reason for the quiet soon revealed itself.

A dead man lay in the open doorway. A bullet had ripped off the top of his head. Another had blasted his right eye to bloody pulp. Flies were crawling all over the dead face. Bodie dismounted and went inside the hut. The interior looked as if a tornado had hit it. Furniture and utensils were thrown everywhere. The area around the cooking stove was littered with spilled food and the cupboard where supplies had been kept was empty. Bodie had one of his questions answered. Reefer had got his food. He had also filled another of his needs, too.

In the corner of the hut, hunched up against the flaking adobe wall, a naked girl watched Bodie through tear-misted eyes. She was around twenty-two years old, with short-cropped tawny hair. Probably pretty, too, Bodie decided. It was hard to tell right there and then because someone had given her a brutal beating around her face. Her lips were split and puffy. There was a huge bruise over her left cheekbone. Dried blood caked her nostrils. A pair of ragged scratches ran from her left shoulder, across the ripe swell of her right breast, tapering off near her groin. Dark bruises marked the white flesh of her body and the curving length of her thighs. At the base of her flat belly the triangle of tawny pubic hair was matted and bloody.

As Bodie approached her the girl lifted a hand, as if to defend herself. The mist left her eyes and they glowed with an intense anger and rage, green and cold.

"Not again!" she said. "Damn you, no! Not again!"

"Ease off, girl," Bodie advised. "I ain't with those two. I'm after the bastards!"

The girl stared at him while she absorbed his words. After a while her hand dropped and her head sagged down on her breasts. She began to cry, softly, her naked shoulders heaving. Bodie left her to it. There was nothing he could do for her at that moment.

He went outside and found a shovel. Choosing a spot he began to dig. By the time he'd finished it was full dark and he was sweating from his exertions. He made his way back to the hut. Going inside he found a lamp and lit it, placing it on the table. Glancing over his shoulder he saw that the girl was still in the corner of the hut.

"Who was he?" he asked.

The girl raised her head, staring at the dark shape lying in the open door.

"My father," she said. "Sam McCoy was his name." She ran a hand through her tangled hair. "They killed him!" she said abruptly, her voice devoid of emotion. "Shot him down like he was nothing! Came in here and tore the place apart looking for money and food! And then they . . . they took me! Ripped my clothes off and beat me when I fought them! What did they expect me to do? Stand there and let them . . . let them . . . do it! They were like animals! Laughing, watching each other do it, over and over! And then they made me . . . !" She broke off, wiping her swollen lips with her hands as if she was trying to rub off some vile taste.

"I've dug a grave," Bodie said. "You want to see?"

The girl stood up, swaying unsteadily. She lifted her head, brushing damp hair back from her bruised face. "I got to get dressed," she said, as if she had only just become aware of her nakedness. She crossed the hut, tall now she was standing, full young breasts trembling tautly as she moved, brown nipples jutting erect against the early evening chill. As she moved by him, Bodie saw more livid scratches marking the white curve of her back, cruelly following the round swell of her firm buttocks. She vanished in a dark corner of the hut, emerging shortly with a blanket over her arm and a bundle of clothes over the other. "I want to bathe first," she said, and walked out of the hut. Bodie followed carrying the lamp. He trailed the girl to the creek, watched her drop her bundle on the bank and then step into the clear water. He heard her gasp as she entered the cold water. Even so she waded out to the centre of the stream, lowering herself until she was able to duck her head under. She came up spluttering, then rose and washed her pale body, wincing as her finger passed over the scratched and bruised flesh. Finished, she emerged from the creek, water spilling from her long legs, gleaming on her trembling breasts. She took the blanket and used it to dry herself. Then she unrolled the bundle of clothes and dressed in a pair of faded old Levi's that were too small across the hips. She pulled on a man's grey shirt, high-heeled boots. She buckled the wide belt holding up the Levi's, then stared at Bodie, her bruised face somehow softened by the yellow light from the lamp.

"Can we bury him now?" she asked.

Bodie gave her the lamp to hold while he wrapped her father's body in a blanket. He picked up the blanketed corpse in his arms and carried it to the hole he'd dug. Lowering the body into the grave, Bodie picked up the shovel and began to fill the hole.

The girl watched him for a while, then she began to sing. Her voice faltered over the first few words, but then it grew stronger as she continued. Bodie recognised the hymn. It was 'Rock of Ages.' The girl sang it through without pause, her strong, clear voice rising to the night sky, floating up towards the pale, cold stars showing against the eternal darkness.

Bodie finished filling in the grave. He gathered some loose rocks and laid them over the mound of earth. The girl watched him in silence until he had finished, then she turned to him and said: "Thank you for what you've done . . . Mr?"

"Bodie."

The girl nodded. "I'm Dana McCoy. You say you're after those two men? Are you a lawman?"

Bodie sleeved sweat from his face. "In a matter of speaking. I'm after Hoyt Reefer and Jim Tyree for the bounty on them."

"They deserve hunting down," Dana exclaimed bitterly. "I hope you make them die real slow! And if that isn't the kind of thing a young woman should say then I don't give a damn, Bodie! Not a damn!"

They returned to the hut. Dana set to and did what she could to clear up the mess. Then she got a fire going in the stove. Bodie brought in his sack of supplies and his coffee and placed them on the table.

"Help yourself," he told Dana.

Soon she had bacon sizzling in the pan and coffee bubbling in a pot. She rescued a loaf of bread from the floor and cut off the soiled crust.

"Isn't much," she said to Bodie when she finally served it up. She somehow made the remark sound like an apology.

"Anything's good when the alternative is nothing," Bodie remarked, helping himself to a thick slice of bread. "You make this?"

Dana nodded, not lifting her eyes from the plate. "My mother taught me. She taught me everything before she died. Then there was just me and . . . " She choked back the words. Her head came up and she stared angrily at Bodie. "Why is this such a cruel land? My father came here twenty years ago. He built this place out of the wilderness. He had to fight to keep it. Indians. Drought. Flood. Sickness. You name it and my father faced it and beat it. When he went away to the War, me and my mother kept the place together. It was hard but we did it. Three times we fought off Comanches. In the end they left us alone. Now it's all over. Ain't nobody but me and I just don't care anymore. There ain't anything else bad can happen to me after today."

Bodie drained his coffee cup and poured himself some more. He spooned in some sugar.

"Trouble with life is it just keeps rolling along. Either you go with it or you just lie down and die. I figure you to be the kind who wouldn't put up with being by the wayside, Dana McCoy."

She looked at him for a long time. Then a faint gleam showed in her deep green eyes. "I don't know where you've come from and I'm sure you're the kind of man my father would have run off his land, Mr Bodie, but I think I like you!"

"Sounds to me your father was a smart feller," Bodie said, smiling.

"He was a good man," Dana said warmly. "A good and honest man. And I dare bet there are few of those about in this country."

"Amen to that!"

After the meal Dana cleared the table. Bodie went outside and put his horse in the corral. He hung his saddle over the top rail. Closing the gate he stood for a moment, breathing in the soft, sage-scented air. There were times, though few, when this wild, savage country, contrary to its nature, revealed a hidden beauty. Fleeting moments of calm. Often brutally shattered, Bodie thought, as he went inside the hut.

"In the morning you'll go after those men?" Dana said.

Bodie nodded. "Yeah."

"I want to ride with you, Bodie," she said calmly. "As far as you have to go and for as long as it takes!"

"No!" Bodie snapped. "Those ain't a couple of old ladies I'm after! Jesus, you ought to know that! I've got enough trailing those two without have you on my tail!"

"Don't try and beat me down with hard words, Bodie! I was born and raised in this country. I know it like the back of my hand, clear down to the border. I can ride as good as any Comanche and shoot a damn sight better. And I don't need reminding what those two are like. I won't let myself forget what they did to me. Not until the pair of them are dead."

"Well don't worry on that score," Bodie said. "I ain't plannin' on taking them in alive!"

Dana stood with her hands on her hips, legs braced apart as she stared him out. "You can say no all night, Bodie, but I aim to go with you! Leave me and I'll follow. Let me ride along and I won't get in your way. You give the orders. I won't hinder you."

Bodie swore under his breath, knowing he was good and trapped. He didn't doubt that she was capable of following him. He wouldn't lose her, not in a country that had been her backyard since she'd been a child. He would only waste his breath trying to talk her out of it. Dana McCoy was a determined, stubborn young woman, and Bodie, from past experience, knew better than to try and make her change her mind.

"Let's get some sleep," he growled.

"I aim to move with the first light!"

She turned and crossed to close the door. "You can have the cot in the corner there," she said, indicating the homemade bed. "I'm over there on the far side of the stove. Goodnight, Mr Bodie."

"Beunos noches, Miss McCoy!"

A little later, wrapped in his blanket, Bodie rolled over, staring across the darkened hut. He was sure he'd heard a faint sound coming from Dana's cot. The sound was low, muffled. It could have been the wind outside. Then again it could have been the lonely cry of a young girl, alone in the world and not yet sure which way to go. Bodie listened for a while and then lay back, letting sleep drug his mind.

12

THEY had made good time since leaving the ranch. The wind of the previous day had gone and the trail they were following was clear. Dawn had merged with the day, the sun climbing swiftly, and by mid-morning the heat was unbearable. Bodie's shirt clung damply to his broad back. Sweat trickled down his face, stinging his eyes. He rode in silence, concentrating on the tracks left by the two horses carrying Reefer and Tyree.

Just behind him Dana McCoy trailed along on a wiry black and white pony. Dana had a battered old cavalry hat pulled down over her eyes. In the cracked scabbard on her saddle rested a well-used Spencer carbine. Dangling from the saddlehorn was a large, filled canteen. Dana herself rode in pained silence. Her bruised body was taut, stiff, aching badly. The bruises on her face had turned dark with blotches of yellow. Her lower lip remained swollen, though the upper lip had gone down well. Sweat glistened on her face, pale beneath her tan. Her shirt had a wide 'V' shape of sweat at the back. It clung wetly to her full breasts in front, emphasising the ripe fullness, her sensitive nipples constantly being chaffed by the shirt's coarse material.

In the long hours since leaving the ranch she and Bodie had barely exchanged a word. Dana didn't try to draw him into a conversation. He would talk when he was ready and not before.

They moved warily along the dry, sandy bed of some long gone creek. The heat, trapped by the sloping banks, reached out and struck them with physical force. Heatwaves shimmered along the length of the barren channel. It glanced off the bright metal of Bodie's Winchester.

He reined in abruptly, swinging the

Winchester to readiness as he saw something ahead of them. A dark, humped shape in the middle of the channel.

"Bodie?" Dana questioned, peering at the distant shape herself.

He silenced her with a sharp flick of his hand. "A goddam horse!"

And so it was. Still saddled, it lay on its side, rigid legs thrust out from its swollen belly. Now Bodie could see the dark blood streaking its mouth and nostrils. A ragged hole showed where a gun had been used to end its life. Flies, thick and black, crawled over the carcass.

Bodie let his eyes move back and forth along the silent, seemingly empty rims of both banks. Nothing moved. There was no sound. But his instincts told him not to be taken in by mere appearance.

"Bodie!"

He continued to scan the rims, letting his horse walk forward, closer to the dead horse.

"Bodie, listen! That horse. It's one of theirs. I recognise it."

The flies, suddenly aware of Bodie's closeness, rose in a buzzing, angry cloud. Hovering, darting, they waited for the intruder to leave so they could resume their feeding.

"Damn you, Bodie, they could still be around"!" Dana persisted.

And I know where, Bodie acknowledged silently, picking the gleam of sunlight as it darted along the barrel of a rifle up on the rim to his left.

"Down!" he yelled over his shoulder at Dana, twisting himself from the saddle as he spoke, and hoping she had the presence to act on his warning.

He was barely clear of the saddle when his ears picked up the distant slam of a shot. The ground rushed up to meet him and he hit on his right shoulder, rolling frantically. As he touched the ground he heard the shrill cry of a horse in pain. Then he was gathering his jangled sense, jerking his body round. He threw the rifle to his shoulder and fired at the drift of powdersmoke up on the rim. His bullet whacked up a gout of earth and he was rewarded by the sight of a blurred figure jerking upright, pulling back from the rim. Bodie levered another round into the breech and fired again but the figure had gone.

He threw a quick glance towards Dana's horse, saw that the saddle was empty. She was down in the sand, the Spencer carbine clasped in her slender hands. Her hat had gone and the tawny cap of hair clung damply to her head.

"Stay down!" he snapped, glowering at her, annoyed by the fact that he had been forced into the position of having to look out for her.

A ragged sound broke the silence. Bodie glanced to his right. His own horse lay on its side, a pulpy hole in its neck where the bullet intended for Bodie had exited. Bodie swore bitterly. He had owned the horse for a good time and it had carried him a long way. He reached down and slid his

Colt from the holster. Levelling it he fired once, putting a .45 bullet through the horse's brain.

The sound of the shot galvanised the hidden rifleman into action. His dark shape appeared briefly, further along the rim from where he'd fired his first shot. Riflefire added to the rattling echo of Bodie's pistol shot. Bullets slammed into the earth around Bodie's prone body. He moved promptly, squirming across the hot sand until he was sheltered by the carcass of his dead horse.

"Dana, get over here, and fast!" Bodie urged. He lifted his rifle and pumped a couple of quick shots in the general direction of the ambusher, giving Dana time to reach his side.

She pushed herself tightly up against the dead horse's underbelly, closing her mind to its sweaty odour.

"I can think of better places to get cosy," she said pointedly.

Bodie ignored her. He was busy thumbing fresh cartridges into the

Winchester. His eyes travelled along the rim, watching for a sign that the ambusher was about to make another try. Come on, you son of a bitch, he begged silently. Show your ass for one lousy second and I'll ream it out with a bullet!

"Where's the other one?" Dana whispered.

"How the hell am I supposed to know? If you're so damn interested wriggle your butt round and keep a watch along the rim behind us."

She did as he suggested without a word and for a time there was a deathly silence. Bodie and the girl could have been the only humans within a hundred miles. It seemed that way, but Bodie knew better. Somewhere close by were Reefer and Tyree. He knew it as sure as he knew that he was going to end up killing the pair of them.

Bodie felt a slight irritation building up. He didn't like the situation. Sitting out in the open, virtually pinned down by a man he couldn't even see. He felt a runnel of sweat trickle down his face and shook it away angrily. Damn! Reefer and Tyree could keep him here until hell froze over if they wanted. He knew that if he dared to put his nose out from behind the dead horse he was liable to have it shot off. But he wasn't going to sit here all day! Somehow, soon, he had to precipitate the action.

"Dana, how good are you with the carbine?" he asked, the germ of an idea growing in his mind.

Dana didn't take her eyes from the slope she was watching. "Give me a clear shot and I'll hit whatever's in my sights!" There was no glib tone to her voice. She was simply stating fact. Bodie believed her.

"If I can get the feller up on the rim to show himself again — can you take him?"

"Just try me, Bodie."

"I aim to, lady, so don't you make a fool of me!"

Dana turned slowly, resting the

Spencer across the carcass of the horse. She eased back the hammer. Glancing at Bodie, her green eyes glittering with feline anticipation, she said: "You going to sit there all day, Mister Bodie?"

Bodie allowed himself a wry smile. He half-rose, stepping out from the cover provided by the dead horse. A feeling of complete nakedness swept over him as he took a quick step forward, hoping that he was giving a convincing exhibition. Another step, then a third, and he was out in the open, as unprotected as a fly on a bare wall. Bodie wondered fleetingly if he'd done the right thing. But it was too late for quitting now. Come on, he swore angrily under his breath. Show yourself, you contrary son of a bitch! And then, out of the corner of his eye, he caught a flicker of movement on the ridge. Sunlight glinting on the menacing rifle barrel. Bodie experienced a strong desire to turn back for the cover of the dead horse. Instead he kept moving forward, making for the base of the slope. With every passing second, each one stretching to what seemed an eternity, Bodie anticipated the crash of a shot, the sudden burst of pain, the paralysing shock. Nothing came. From the ambusher's rifle — or from Dana's. What the hell was she playing at? Surely she'd had time to fire! Maybe all she'd told him had been fantasy! Jesus, maybe she didn't even know how to operate the damn rifle! He was going to look a real . . . !

The flat, hard sound of the shot caught him unaware. Bodie felt his body tense, waiting for the bullet to hit. But then the realisation came. The shot had come from behind him. From Dana's Spencer! Bodie threw a quick glance up towards the ridge and saw the ambusher slither over the edge, rolling, bouncing, tumbling, helplessly down the sandy slope. He hit bottom with a sudden smack, his head twisted at an odd angle. Even from where he was standing Bodie could see the pulpy hole the Spencer's bullet had blown through the man's chest and out between his shoulders.

He turned, seeing Dana, a wide smile on her bruised face, standing up. Bodie waved her down. He hadn't forgotten there had been two of them. The brief look he'd had at the face of the man Dana had just shot had confirmed him to be Tyree. That meant Hoyt Reefer was still alive and free, and if he was around he could show himself at any moment.

He spotted a flicker of movement partway up the slope behind Dana. Saw a dusty figure step out from behind a half-buried rock, rifle already lifting. Bodie knew the face. Hoyt Reefer! The man who had led the bunch of renegade killers Bodie had been tracking down.

"Dana, get down!" Bodie yelled. He lunged forward, bringing his rifle up as he moved.

She had stared at him for a second or two. Fragments of time that were far too long. Hoyt Reefer's rifle blasted a gout of flame.

Dana's smile vanished in a wide-eyed look of pure terror as Reefer's bullet ripped through her body. It went in just at the top of her right shoulder, angling downwards to emerge from her left breast in a burst of bloody flesh. The front of her shirt was drenched in blood as she flopped forward across the carcass of the dead horse. Her face twisted round towards Bodie and he could see the blood gouting from her slack mouth. Her body twitched in ugly spasms of approaching death.

The moment Reefer's rifle had fired Bodie levelled his own Winchester. He triggered one shot that missed, but which passed close enough to Reefer to startle him. The renegade, his unshaven face darkened even more by his wild scowl, yanked his weapon round and worked the lever frantically. His finger was just beginning to ease back on the trigger when Bodie fired a second time. The bullet clipped Reefer's left arm, gouging a raw furrow through the flesh. Reefer grunted, jerked wildly on the trigger of his rifle, sending a bullet into the dirt at Bodie's feet. Bodie launched himself forward, hitting the ground belly down, rolling off to one side before he thrust his rifle out and up at Reefer's body. He touched the trigger, felt the rifle jerk as it fired, then saw Hoyt Reefer step back as the bullet punched a ragged hole in his side. Blood began to spread across Reefer's shirt. Before the renegade could react Bodie fired again, then put four more bullets into Reefer's twisting body. Each bullet tore its own bloody hole. Reefer's front was drenched in pulsing scarlet. He made a supreme effort to fire his own weapon again. Bodie, up on one knee, took what seemed to be a terrible deliberation over the last shot. When it came the sound rolled out along the dry creek bed, echoing briefly before fading into silence. The bullet took Hoyt Reefer just forward of his left ear, the angle of the shot taking it up through his skull, into the sensitive, delicate mass of the brain. Reefer's body, already dead, took a final step forward down the slope, lost all control and plunged face down on the blood-spattered sand.

Bodie stood up slowly, gazing about him. He reloaded his Winchester and then went across to where Dana lay across the dead horse. He eased her down to the ground. She was still breathing though very faintly. Bodie opened her shirt and examined the wound. He knew at a glance that there was nothing he could do for her. The bullet had done too much damage during its flight through her body. The left breast had been mutilated badly and there was too much blood still flowing from her body.

Dana's eyes opened slowly and she stared at Bodie from the green depth. Finally she recognised him and tried to smile. "Hey . . . Bodie . . . I got him . . . for you. Just like I said I would . . . !"

"Never doubt a lady's word," Bodie said.

She nodded slowly. "You get . . . the . . . other?"

"Hoyt Reefer? Yeah, he's dead! They're all dead, Dana McCoy."

Dana sighed deeply, screwing up her bloody face in agony. "We're all dead then, Mr Bodie," she murmured.

Bodie figured she was rambling, but when he glanced down at her a few seconds later he realised what she had meant. Her eyes were closed and her faint breathing had ceased. Hell, Bodie thought, she was right. They are all dead!

Except you! he told himself. He stood up and stared about him. Wasn't that always the way? They always ended up dead. He was always left alive — but alone! Always, always alone!

13

HE buried Dana as well as he was able, covering the shallow grave he'd dug with his bare hands with heavy stone. A waste of life, he thought, walking away from the mounded earth. But at least she'd got her revenge, and that could mean a lot to someone who had been badly hurt. Later he located the remaining horse that had belonged to the renegades. He wrapped Reefer and Tyree in blankets and draped them across the horse's back, tying them down. After that he made a small fire and cooked himself a quick meal, brewed some coffee.

He would ride Dana's mount, and lead the horse carrying the stiffening corpses of Reefer and Tyree. San Antonio lay a good two days' ride away. Bodie settled himself in his saddle for a steady ride. He wasn't in any kind of hurry.

A couple of hours later he realised that he was not alone after all. The feeling had been lurking at the back of his mind ever since the night he'd been disturbed in his camp. And there had been the strange killings too. The fact that he had been put out of action before Kelly's murder. The more Bodie thought about the separate incidents the more certain he became of some kind of conspiracy. Awareness of it made little difference if he was in the dark as to the reason behind it all. And that annoyed Bodie. He liked to have his problems out in the open. In clear daylight where he could see just who was set against him.

He began to take careful notice of his surroundings. The feeling of being shadowed grew stronger. Bodie knew without having to actually see them, that there was more than one. Outwardly he rode casually, making no sudden moves to warn his unseen adversaries. Beneath the surface his mind and body seethed with activity. Eyes moved back and forth, searching every shadow, checking every hollow, following every dusty ridge. His ears listened for a warning sound, tiny, whispered intonation. His very being was primed, rigid, taut. He knew that whoever these people were they wanted him dead!

Dead and buried and forgotten!

The sun rose higher in the shimmering sky, the pulsing orb drawing the very life from the parched earth. It reached its apex and hovered, as though waiting for some event to take place before it began the long westward slide into night.

Bodie eased his horse across a sandy slope dotted with tangled mesquite. Solitary cacti dotted the terrain, poised and oddly menacing as they posed against the far-distant haze of the horizon.

He heard the soft, nervous sound of a horse blowing through its nostrils. The sound was abruptly cut off and

Bodie could imagine a rough hand being clamped across the animal's muzzle. The sound had come from somewhere off to Bodie's right. It was all the warning he needed!

Snatching his rifle from its place on his saddle, Bodie kicked his feet free from the stirrups and rolled off his horse's back. He threw out a hand to break his fall, letting his body curve and roll. He heard the sudden blast of a shot. Gritty sand misted the air around him as his horse, alarmed by the shot, broke into a wild gallop. It went down the slope, dragging the other horse with it.

Bodie got his feet under him and ran, crouching as low as he could. He had seen a deep hollow in the ground ahead of him and that was where he was heading. The flat smack of gunshots followed him. He heard bullets whack the ground around him. Nothing touched him until the instant before he reached the edge of the hollow.

He felt the bullet tip its way across his back, then bite deeper through the fleshy part of his left arm, just below the shoulder. The impact of the bullet spun him round. Bodie went over the rim of the hollow and hit the slope near its base, some ten feet below. He struggled to his feet, ignoring the burning pain in his back and arm. He could sense the wetness of blood running down his arm, soaking his shirt, but he didn't have the time to do anything about it.

At the far end of the deep hollow lay a mass of tangled thorn and mesquite and brush. Bodie ran towards it. There was no way of telling just how deep the heavy brush might go, but it was the only chance he had of gaining any kind of cover. He plunged into the thick brush, paying no mind to the vicious thorns clawing at his clothes and the flesh beneath. A few scratches were preferable than a bullet in the back. Above the dry rattle of the brush as he forced his way through

Bodie heard raised voices. They must have seen him go over the edge of the hollow. It wouldn't take them long to figure out where he'd gone. Once that happened they would pick up his trail and start to track him again.

It was a turnabout, Bodie thought wryly — the stalker being stalked! But they weren't going to find him patiently sitting and waiting for the end. Hell, no! Whatever it was they wanted they were going to pay dearly! In blood!

The tangled, knotted forest of brush and thorn seemed to spread forever. Here and there cane breaks rose out of the intertwined mass of brush. Dwarf trees grew alongside tornillo and blackjack, a green canopy over Bodie's head as he moved on through the maze of vegetation. The Mexicans called this green hell the brasada. The great islands of thorny brush could go on for miles. It was easy to get lost in such places. In cattle country the brasada was a favorite place for the wandering longhorns. The steers loved the cool shade offered by the greenery and once in there it was no mean feat to get them out.

The brasada was also home to the javelina, a vicious, bloodthirsty wild hog which had little respect for any living creature. Armed with razor-sharp tusks and enviable speed, the javelina would charge a man without hesitation. It had a nasty disposition and a habit of attacking without a moment's warning.

Crouching in the shadow of some thick scrub Bodie listened to the distant sound of his pursuers. The mass of the brasada had the irritating effect of breaking up sounds, making it difficult to pinpoint where a given shout originated. Bodie sat back and let the sounds come closer. Somewhere he could hear a man on a horse. The brush crackled and popped as the heavy bulk of the horse pushed its way through. Bodie heard the man swear as sharp thorns ripped his flesh, drawing blood. Peering into the twisted mass of vegetation Bodie spotted the approaching bulk of man and horse. He rose to his feet and moved forward, coming to a natural break in the brush, and as Bodie stepped into the open on one side the rider broke through on the other.

They saw each other in the same moment. The rider, a broad, squat man with a full belly hanging over his belt, dropped his reins and tried to lift the rifle he was carrying in his left hand. He was far too slow. Bodie's Winchester swung up, blasting flame and smoke. The rider let out a hurt yell as Bodie's bullet ripped a chunk of flesh from his left shoulder. Blood began to soak the rider's grubby blue shirt. Bodie's rifle cracked again. The rider's head was jerked round by the terrible force of the bullet. A shower of blood streamed down over the rider's face, clogging his eyes. Not that it made any difference, because by the time he hit the ground the rider was dead.

Bodie ran towards the dead man's

horse. The animal startled by the gunfire and the smell of blood, backed off. In his haste Bodie made a wild grab for the trailing reins. His abrupt movement made the horse bolt. It crashed off through the brush, tearing its sides on the vicious thorns.

"Over there! He's over there! Dammit, I heard the goddam shooting!"

The voice was close. Bodie thumbed fresh bullets into his Winchester, noting that they were the last ones in his pocket. He moved towards the dead man, preparing to check his pockets. Then a shot crashed out. The bullet ripped through the brush, splintering tall canes, showering Bodie with needle-like slivers.

"I see him! Over here, you assholes!"

Bodie turned and plunged out of the clearing, deep into the clawing, thorny depths of the brasada. He felt something gouge the side of his face. Felt hot blood stream down his cheek from a laceration. Behind him he could hear the heavy crash of a horse being forced through the thick brush. The animal was making its protests heard, but its rider drove in his heels, yelling wildly at the top of his lungs.

"Hey, hey, you sons of bitches! I got the bastard on the run! Look at him go!"

That was the moment when Bodie stopped running, turned on his heels, and shot the yelling, grinning man out of the saddle. Bodie's bullet hit him chest-high, spinning the man off to one side. He smashed bodily against an upthrust growth of cane he had just ridden his horse through. There was a moment's silence and then a long, terrible scream of agony as the man's body slid down onto the spears of the cane. The needle points of splintered cane penetrated the soft flesh, pushing deeper as the weight of the man's squirming body bore him down. The screaming died off in a wet gurgle as blood rose in the dying man's throat.

"Jesus!"

"What the hell's goin' on?"

"Harry? Damn you, Harry, where are you?"

Smiling grimly Bodie eased his way deeper into the brasada. Maybe now they would think twice before they came again.

He moved through the thick brush for long minutes. When there were no more sounds he took time to rest. On his heels he gently exercised his arm, feeling the soft pulse of pain. The wound needed seeing to, but there was no chance of that out here. He reached across with his right hand, carefully probing the ragged tear in his flesh. His fingers came away sticky with congealing blood. Only now did he feel a slight sickness, reaction to the damage done by the bullet. He stayed where he was, making the most of his chance to rest, giving his weary body an opportunity to recover.

He had been right about one thing. The bastards certainly wanted him dead. If the chance arose he wanted to get one of them alive. There were questions Bodie needed to ask. Like who wanted him dead. And why. He had enemies, of that he was acutely aware. Who amongst them might suddenly decide Bodie needed killing? A faint grin edged his mouth. Knowing his enemies as he did that could cover them all?

Bodie jerked upright, blinking his eyes. Damn! He rubbed his face. He'd almost drifted into sleep. The heat of the sun, sifting down through the green canopy, hung over him like a smothering blanket. Bodie licked his dry lips. He thought of his canteen, hanging from his saddle. It might as well have been a thousand miles away the good it was going to do him. Shading his eyes with his hand Bodie squinted up through the canopy of greenery over his head. He watched the sun for a moment, then slumped back, frowning. There were too many long hours before darkness. He wasn't going to be able to sit back and wait for the dark.

His ears caught a faint rustling in the brush off to his left. Bodie snatched up his rifle and edged back into the brush at his back. He heard the sound again. A dark shape emerged from the criss-cross shadows deeper in the brush. Bodie made out the tall shape of a dark-skinned halfbreed. Clad in faded, tight Levi's that moulded themselves to powerful, muscled thighs and knee-high Apache moccasins, his lithe body naked from the waist up, the breed edged from the brush. He paused, bright, keen eyes searching, head cocked as he listened. Bodie judged him to be part Apache and part Mexican. Black hair and glittering obsidian eyes. High cheekbones. The lips thick and flat below the hook nose. The breed's only weapon, apart from the knife tucked down one of his moccasins, was a Winchester with a cut-down stock and a short barrel.

Bodie knew the odd looking rifle well. He also knew its owner.

The breed was known as Silverbuck.

His name had come from his insistence in being paid in silver dollars for any work he did. Like killing a man. Or two men. Or however many men needed killing. Silverbuck never complained. He was good at his work. A silent, deadly, unfeeling killer for hire.

The last time Bodie had faced Silverbuck it had almost resulted in one of them dying. Because the man Bodie had been tracking, for a long time, had turned out to be Silverbuck's employer at the time. The breed had been prepared to kill Bodie to safeguard his investment. In the end the only one to die had been the man Bodie had been after. He had stepped in the way of Silverbuck's bullet, intended for Bodie. The distraction had given Bodie time to gain cover. But by the time he had shown himself again Silverbuck had gone, deciding that with his employer dead there was little to be gained from staying around.

Watching the prowling breed Bodie felt the old anger rising. He could imagine Silverbuck's pleasure when he had been offered money to go out and kill Bodie. Let's see you try, you bastard! Bodie slid his rifle forward, following Silverbuck's progress. He raised the muzzle a fraction, felt the barrel snag against a hanging tendril of thorn. The slight movement was enough to create a whisper of sound. Instantly Silverbuck reacted, his dark body twisting round, lowering to a crouch. The stubby rifle came round too, arcing towards Bodie's place of concealment. The black muzzle winked flame and a gush of smoke. The sound of the shot rattled across the clearing. Bodie felt the wind of the bullet as it passed his face. He cursed softly, rolling away from his position, trying to pull himself deeper into the brush. Silverbuck's rifle cracked again. He kept firing as he ran forward. Bullets ripped through the brush around Bodie. He knew that eventually one of those bullets was going to find him.

"This time I kill you, Bodie!"

Silverbuck's taunt floated through the haze of powdersmoke. A harsh laugh filled the air, followed by a long, high howl. "Show yourself, Bodie! I am Silverbuck and this day I will kill you!"

Bodie rose up on one knee, hugging the Winchester to his shoulder. Just keep talking, you son of a bitch, he begged. Make all the noise you want cause it gives me something to shoot at. He held Silverbuck's weaving figure in his sights through the tangled web of brush, easing back on the trigger. The Winchester cracked and Silverbuck's taunting cry changed to a hurt yelp. He clapped his hand to his side, feeling the hot blood, and realising his lack of caution threw himself to one side as Bodie fired again.

The second shot had missed, Bodie knew. He thrust to his feet, shouldering his way through the brush, stepping out into the open. He searched the area for a sign of the halfbreed. There was a sudden rush of sound close by his right side. Bodie twisted round just as Silverbuck's hurtling shape crashed against him. The breed had tossed aside his empty rifle, replacing it with the thick-bladed, razor edged knife he carried in his moccasin. Bodie felt himself going down with Silverbucks's writhing body wrapped about him. They hit the ground hard, Silverbuck grunting in triumph. He slashed the knife down at Bodie's throat and met only empty air as the manhunter jerked his head back. Before Silverbuck could bring the knife back for a second cut Bodie, remembering he was still holding his Winchester, jabbed the hard butt of the stock against the side of Silverbuck's face. Silverbuck grunted as the cheek bone cracked. Soft flesh split and blood welled from the ragged gash. Aware of the deadly knife the breed still held Bodie tossed his rifle aside and caught hold of Silverbuck's wrist, forcing the glittering blade away from his body. He shoved the heel of his right hand hard up against the underside of Silverbuck's jaw, pushing the breed's head back. There was a moment of panic and then Silverbuck regained control of his emotions. His left fist hammered down across Bodie's face. Bodie's head rocked to one side, pain flaring in his jaw. Blood streamed from a torn lip. He released his pressure on Silverbuck's jaw, drew his fist back, then clubbed the breed across the mouth. Silverbuck's face twisted in a rictus of agony. He spat blood and broken teeth. Bodie hit him again, crushing Silverbuck's nose. Blood squirted out in streams. Silverbuck wrenched himself away from Bodie, breaking the grip the manhunter had on his wrist. Letting himself roll Silverbuck came to his feet swiftly, thrusting the knife out before him, point uppermost. Yet before he even saw his adversary Bodie was on him. He had come to his feet as the breed had rolled away. The toe of his boot lashed up and out, catching Silverbuck in the stomach. White-hot pain speared his stomach. He stumbled back fighting for breath, tears stinging his eyes as he tried to see Bodie. But there was no chance to see Bodie. The manhunter stepped in close, grasping Silverbuck's knife wrist with one hand. Bodie's other arm slid beneath Silverbuck's arm, just above the elbow joint. Bodie put on the pressure, using Silverbuck's own weight as a lever. He thrust down hard against the arm joint, heard Silverbuck gasp, and thrust again. The arm bone snapped with an audible crack, the bone piercing the flesh of the arm, blood spurting from the wound. Silverbuck gave a low groan and slumped to his knees, the knife slipping forgotten from his hand. Crouching, Bodie picked up the knife. He took hold of a handful of Silverbuck's black hair and yanked the breed's head back, pressing the top of the knife against the taut throat.

"Now listen to me, you halfbreed son of a bitch!" Bodie pressed on the knife so that the top penetrated the flesh, letting a thin runnel of blood run down the breed's throat and across his naked chest. "Don't play games with me! All I want from you is the name of the bastard who set you on my trail! Start remembering fast, cause you ain't got much time left!"

Silverbuck tried to twist his body away from Bodie. All that happened was that the blade of the knife sliced into his throat. Just deep enough to make the blood flow steadily.

"You keep wrigglin' about like that and you'll end up cutting your own throat," Bodie said coldly. "That would disappoint me somethin' awful, Silverbuck, cause I want to do the cuttin' myself."

"Go to hell, you bastard!" Silverbuck hissed through clenched teeth. Sweat gleamed on his set, bronze face. He stared up at Bodie through eyes burning with hatred. "I don't tell you a thing!"

Bodie slammed his right knee up into Silverbuck's face. He heard something crunch and as Silverbuck sagged back, blood gushed from his mouth.

Silverbuck's head dropped against his chest. Blood streamed down his naked torso, soaking his pants. Still angry, Bodie hit the breed again, his fist coming down like a club. The blow struck Silverbuck across the back of his neck and he flopped face down on the ground, jerking softly, like a landed fish. Bodie planted a brutal knee in Silverbuck's back, took hold of his hair again and yanked the breed's head up off the ground. Dirt had ground itself into the open gashes, clung to the sticky blood. Silverbuck's eyes rolled, uncoordinated. He hardly seemed aware of his surroundings. Bodie pressed the keen edge of the knife against the rigid line of his throat.

"Who hired you, Silverbuck?"

Silverbuck spat blood. He began to dribble pink froth. "F—— you, Bodie! You wan' kill me? Then go 'head!"

Bodie rammed his knee down hard. He heard Silverbuck's ribs crack. A low groan bubbled past the breed's lips. "He must be payin' you a lot, Silverbuck! You figure it's worth it?"

"I ain't tellin' you a damn thing, Bodie!" Silverbuck's voice rose to a shrill protest, and it didn't stop until the blade of the knife in Bodie's hand sliced its way across his throat, laying it open. Silverbuck kicked and jerked for a time. Only when he was still did Bodie let the breed's head drop.

He stood up, still holding the bloody knife, and gazed down at the bloody corpse. Turning away to pick up his rifle Bodie murmured. "Silverbuck, it seems like I've gone and cashed you in!"

Then he picked up his rifle and went looking for the rest of the bunch who had been sent to kill him. He had quit running from them. He had murder in his heart and no thought of mercy for any of them. He was no longer the hunted!

Now he was the hunter!

He was Bodie — The Stalker!

14

THERE were two more.

Bodie took them both without even raising a sweat. It was like competing against five year old kids. He killed the first one with a .45 bullet through the back of the head, coming up behind the man without being heard or seen. The man had died with an extremely surprised expression on what was left of his face.

The last one was just as easy. He tried to put up a fight, but Bodie put a quick shot through his left kneecap, blowing the joint apart, and after that the man was only too willing to talk. He told everything he knew, and when he'd finished the look in Bodie's eyes was terrible to see. The man had begged for help. Bodie's knee shot had crippled him. He was in great pain and losing a lot of blood. Bodie obliged, putting a bullet between the man's eyes to end his suffering.

Bodie helped himself to ammunition from the dead men's saddlebags. He took what food and water he could find, then used one of the stray horses to make his way back to where he had abandoned his own mount.

He put the supplies he'd gathered into his saddlebags, cut free the horse carrying the dead Reefer and Tyree, and mounted up. Turning the animal towards San Antonio Bodie rode on, leaving the scattered corpses to the already circling vultures.

He rode without pause. He drank water from the canteen on the move, chewed dried beef. When he came to water he stopped only long enough to let his horse drink. Then he rode on. He was tired and bloody and battered. He ached in every joint. Yet he rode like some grim spectre through the long dark night hours and into the next day, ignoring the pre-dawn chill and the burning heat of the new day.

He sighted San Antonio in the early afternoon. Riding on he passed through the busy town, paying no attention to the curious stares he was getting from the citizens of the thriving community. As the noise of San Antonio slipped into the background, Bodie's whole being focused on the gleaming railroad tracks curving off across the dusty Texas landscape. About half a mile out of town was a spurline, and sitting on that spurline was the end of Bodie's trail.

The black and maroon locomotive looked just the same as it had the day Bodie had first seen it. So did the long, richly-decorated Pullman.

As Bodie approached the coach he saw the men lounging around in the blazing sunlight. He saw them for what they were. Hired guns. Bleak faced, with that hungry look in their cold eyes. Nervous hands never far away from the jutting handles of the guns they wore like primitive objects of religion. As they saw him coming they broke apart and formed a human barrier between him and the Pullman.

Bodie reined in and dismounted,

"You're a dead man, Bodie," one of them said, smiling as if he had just said something funny.

His partners grinned too. They were confident. They figured they had it made. That they were going to be the ones to gun down Bodie. The man they called The Stalker. So Bodie let them go on thinking that.

And while they thought he drew his Colt and started shooting.

He took the leader out with his first shot, planting a bullet in the man's smirking face. The expanding .45 bullet burst the man's head open like an over ripe melon.

The moment he'd fired Bodie changed position, moving fast before the other gunmen could react. He snapped off two rapid shots at the closest, blasting a raw hole through the man's side, while his second bullet took out the man's throat, leaving a pulpy hole that spilled blood down the man's shirt.,

The remaining pair managed to get off a couple of shots. One even came within a foot of Bodie's body. It was the closest any of them came. The next shot was Bodie's and it took the man out of the game for good. He went to the ground with a bullet in his heart. The sole survivor stood his ground, reckless confidence spurring him on. He shot off two bullets, both of which went wide of the mark due to his lack of patience in aiming. Even as the final shot was being fired Bodie lifted his Colt, held it steady and pulled the trigger. The Colt jerked in recoil, then steadied for Bodie to use his last shot. It hit the target a fraction of an inch below the first one. The gunman spun round before falling face down on the ground, twin pulpy cones of raw flesh protruding between his shoulders like miniature humps.

Bodie flipped open the loading-gate and began punching out the empty cases. He thumbed in fresh cartridges as he moved towards the Pullman coach.

Steam burst from the locomotive. Dense black smoke surged from the stack. The locomotive surged forward then steadied, couplings clanging.

Thrusting the last bullet into the Colt's cylinder Bodie broke into a run as the Pullman coach began to draw away from him. He should have expected Lyle Trask to have a last card to play. Not that the game was over yet.

The door at the rear of the Pullman was jerked open and a dark-suited figure stepped out onto the swaying observation-platform. Bodie recognised the hard face, the cropped cap of dark hair clinging to the skull. Teal! Lyle Trask's man. He saw something else as well. The stubby shape of a sawn-off shotgun swung in his direction. He heard the boom of one barrel, heard the whistle of the spreading shot. His shoulder struck the dirt and he rolled, coming up on one knee, bringing up his

Colt in a fluid movement. He triggered two quick shots at Teal then thrust to his feet and ran for the Pullman.

Teal ducked low as the shots were fired. One shattered the glass panel of the door at his back. The other clipped the top of his left shoulder, nicking the flesh. Teal stumbled back, off-balance as the floor of the observation-platform rocked under his feet. Throwing out a hand Teal grabbed the rail that ran around the platform and pulled himself upright.

At that moment Bodie reached the Pullman. He caught hold of the rail and jumped for the step. He saw Teal in the act of regaining his feet and lunged up onto the observation platform. He smashed bodily into Teal, driving the cursing man back. They hit the door leading to the Pullman's interior and it splintered under their combined weight, spilling them to the carpeted floor inside. Teal lashed out with booted feet, catching Bodie in the chest and throwing him clear. As Bodie slithered along the panelled wall Teal scrambled to his feet, dragging back the shotgun's second hammer. He swung round to find his target, triggering the charge too soon. The blast of shot ripped a jagged hole in the wall. Seeing that he'd missed Teal plunged forward, swinging the empty shotgun like a club. Bodie, down on one knee, ducked under the vicious swing, then drove the barrel of his Colt into Teal's face. The edge of the sight sliced open Teal's left cheek. Teal grunted in pain. He swung the shotgun again, driving it down across Bodie's gunhand. The Colt slipped from Bodie's numbed fingers. Bodie thrust his left hand out, grabbing hold of Teal's shirt front. He braced himself and swung Teal round. The shirt ripped and Teal was flung across the coach. He hit the far wall, bouncing off, and ran straight into Bodie's rising boot. It sank into Teal's groin, wrenching a high scream from the man. As Teal staggered back Bodie hit him again, blood spurting from Teal's mashed lips. Teal still managed to lift the heavy shotgun, lashing out blindly in Bodie's direction. Bodie swayed his body back out of the way, and as Teal was half-turned by the force of his own swing, Bodie caught hold of his coat and ran him across the floor. Teal let out a terrified yell as he realised where Bodie was directing him. Then it was too late. There was a sudden shattering of glass as Teal smashed headfirst through one of the Pullman's side windows. Bodie kept shoving. There was a moment when Teal got a grip on the frame of the broken window, but then Bodie gave a final heave and Teal went over the edge of the frame. His writhing body twisted frantically as he fell, and when he hit the hard ground his broken body bounced and slithered for yards before coming to rest against an upthrust rock at the side of the track.

Gasping for breath Bodie scooped up his Colt. He replaced the spent cartridges. Then he moved along the Pullman until he reached the door leading to Lyle Trask's private compartment. The door was locked. Bodie unlocked it by the simple procedure of using his boot. The door swung open and Bodie stepped through.

"Glad you were able to make it, Mr Bodie," Lyle Trask smiled from behind his big oak desk.

Bodie booted the door shut behind him. He edged it securely with one of the heavy armchairs.

"Somebody following you, Mr Bodie?" Trask inquired, trying to keep his tone light.

Bodie smiled through bruised, bloody lips. "Not any more, Trask! Not Silverbuck, or any of his crew! Not even Mr Teal! He just got off the train. The hard way.

Trask's face paled a fraction. He didn't speak for a moment and when he finally did his voice was low. "Are you planning a similar fate for me, Bodie!"

Bodie slumped down in an armchair facing Trask, the muzzle of his Colt never once moving off Trask's body.

"You owe me $10,000, Trask! Cash! Now! You sent me after Reefer and his gang. They're all dead. I figure you got the first delivery. Reefer and Tyree are out there somewhere. You want 'em you go and drag 'em in before the vultures finish 'em off."

Trask nodded. "I'll take you word for it." He slid open a drawer in the desk and took out and threw across the desk a thick wad of banknotes. "It's all there. The whole 10,000. Count it if you want. I had a feeling you might be calling in for it so I kept it handy."

"No faith in your own men!" Bodie shook his head. "That's sad, Mister Trask. If a man like you can't buy the best what chance do us poor bastards have?"

"I . . . I . . . don't know what you mean," Trask began lamely. His eyes began to flick about the compartment as if he was looking for a way out. He was beginning to show the symptoms of a trapped man.

Bodie snapped back the Colt's hammer, his anger rising in a burning flood. "The hell you don't, you double-crossing bastard! You set me up! Sent me out to do your dirty work and then hired a bunch of second-rate guns to get rid of me! You miserable son of a bitch! What the hell was it all for?"

"Haven't you worked it out, Bodie?" Trask asked, his control returning slowly.

"Shit, you bastard, I've been too damn busy trying to stay alive to sit down and work out why."

"Simple really, Bodie," Trask said. "You see, years ago, when I first started out, I needed money fast. I wasn't fussy where it came from. So I organised thefts from government warehouses, businesses, freight lines, from anywhere I could locate guns. Those guns were supplied to a bunch who had contacts all along the border country. The main customers were

Comanches. Then there were always the Mexicans. It was a good market. And a very lucrative one too."

"Son of a bitch!" Bodie breathed softly. Suddenly he knew what Trask was leading up to. "Hoyt Reefer was your contact? You ran stolen guns to Reefer!"

"For nearly three years," Trask admitted. "They were hectic years, Bodie, and I wouldn't have missed a second! And they were money-making years too!"

"And now you want to step up in the world," Bodie said wearily. "But it wouldn't do your image any good if the voters found out you were no better than the bad boys you wanted to rid the country of? Am I getting it right, Trask?"

Lyle Trask shrugged his expensively-clad shoulders. "Once Hoyt Reefer got to hear what I was planning to do you think he would of just sat back and let me do it? Bodie, I couldn't take the chance. I needed Reefer's mouth closing for good!" Trask leaned back in his seat. "So I thought why not hire the best man for the job. Let him track Reefer down and wipe him out. It would get rid of my worry over Reefer and also provide me with my political platform.

"You were going to use Reefer and his bunch?"

Trask nodded. "Of course. I was perfectly serious about presenting the dead men as proof of my genuine feelings about lawlessness." Trask managed a wry smile. "It almost worked, Bodie."

"So why the need to have me dead too?" Bodie asked.

"How would I know for certain that Reefer hadn't spilled the beans to you before he died? It was simply a precaution, Bodie. A way of making things all neat and tidy."

"Like Jim Kelly?"

"I almost overlooked him. It was Teal who pointed out that Kelly and Reefer had been in business for some time. Reefer might have talked about me. So

Teal followed you to Anderson's Halt and got rid of Kelly before you could talk to him."

"So Teal was the one. I suppose he killed the girl too. Sherry? You remember?"

"Well I think Teal got a little over enthusiastic there, Bodie. He was worried she might have picked up some information. So he made sure she wouldn't do any talking. It was perhaps a little hasty of him, but he had my best interests at heart!"

"Yeah! Well his interests in everything has kind of died off by now!" Bodie stood up and moved to stand over Trask's desk. He stared at Lyle Trask, his eyes revealing the rage boiling up inside him. "Looks to me, Trask, like you're in the shit all the way up to your neck! Ain't goin' to take very much effort to shove you right under!"

Trask ran his tongue across his dry lips. "Listen, Bodie, it doesn't have to be that way. Hell, man, neither of us are fools! We know the way the world runs. A man has to make his way the best he can. I have a good chance to go far in politics, Bodie, and any man who goes with me could stand to make himself very wealthy. This $10,000 would be chicken feed . . . "

Trask reached out and laid his hand over the wad of notes on the desk. He slid the money across the desk, closer to Bodie.

Bodie's left hand stretched out and his fingers closed over Trask's wrist. He lifted Trask's hand off the money, placing it on the desk top. Trask raised his eyes to Bodie's and smiled confidently. Bodie smiled back. It was a fleeting expression and if Trask had looked deeper he would have realised that it was an emotionless gesture. Trask was still staring into Bodie's eyes when the gun in Bodie's hand came down across his outstretched hand. The fingers of Trask's hand were pulped and crushed as Bodie struck again and again. His left hand, gripping Trask's wrist, held the man's hand in place despite Trask's agonised struggling. Blood squirted from Trask's mangled fingers, spreading across the polished desk top in bright runnels. Trask suddenly opened his mouth to scream. Bodie simply lashed out with the Colt, laying Trask's lips open to the gums, breaking Trask's teeth with a brutal blow. Lyle Trask slumped back in his seat. He hugged his ruined right hand to his chest, moaning softly through his pulped mouth. Blood streamed from the crushed hand, staining Trask's white shirt and suit. It oozed from the ugly gashes in his mouth. Trask stared at Bodie through terror glazed eyes.

"For God's sake, Bodie!" Trask mumbled through his ruined lips. "What are you going . . . to . . . do?"

"Trask, I've got me one rule I never break," Bodie said. "It's helped keep me alive for a long time, and I ain't about to change things now. If a man figures to kill me then he'd better do it first try cause he ain't going to be left in any condition to have a second go.

Trask, you had more than your share of tries. Now it's mine and it's the only one I'll need!"

Lyle Trask realised he was looking death in the face. Despite his terror and the pain he was suffering, he refused to just sit back and die without a fight. With a wild yell he lurched up out of his seat, lashing out at Bodie with his free, uninjured hand, then ran across the compartment to the door at the far end.

Bodie had reached behind him, plucking from a sheath on his belt the knife he's taken from and used on Silverbuck. He reversed the heavy knife, holding it by the top of the blade. Raising his arm he threw it back, then jerked it forward, releasing the knife at the end of the swing. The glittering blade blurred as it made its short journey. It struck home just as Lyle Trask threw a despairing glance over his shoulder. The top of the blade entered Trask's neck on the left side just forward and below the ear, cutting its way through flesh and tendon alike. It penetrated Trask's throat completely, the point emerging on the right side. Blood flowed as Lyle Trask let out a terrified scream. Pain began to burn through the initial shock. Trask stumbled and fell against the compartment wall. His legs began a frantic tattoo, his heels rapping against the floor. A gout of blood spewed from his trembling mouth.

Bodie crossed to Trask's desk and picked up the $10,000. He tucked it in his pants pocket. Turning he went over to where Trask had slumped against the base of the wall. Gripping the handle of the knife Bodie jerked it free. Trask's body arched in silent agony. Bodie wiped the blade of the knife on the expensive carpet that was already stained with Trask's blood.

He reached up and pulled the emergency-cord. Seconds later the coach lurched as the locomotive began to brake, wheels squealing in protest. Bodie waited until the train had come to a halt. He dragged the armchair away from the shattered door and swung it open. He glanced at Trask's motionless body. The blood had stopped flowing now and Trask was still.

"End of the line, Mr Trask," he said. "The train ain't goin' anywhere and neither are you!"

Stepping down from the observation-platform Bodie started walking. It was a fair way back to San Antonio. He figured it would give him time to get his story worked out. Bodie knew damn well that he was going to have some fast, hard explaining to do to the law. One way and another, by the time he'd done he would have earned his $10,000. He wasn't too certain about the $10,000 in bounty money on the Reefer bunch. It might be in his interests to forget about that. The law was going to be hard enough on him over the whole damn mess. Bodie reckoned he could talk his way out of it, but if he started shouting the odds about $10,000 in bounty, somebody, somewhere, might just start getting awkward.

Sometimes, Bodie decided, life had a habit of turning sour on a man. It took hold of him. Turned him upside down and inside out, kicked him from hell to breakfast, and then when he figured he'd had his share of problems it went and gave him a swift kick up the ass just for the hell of it! He shrugged. What the hell! Tomorrow was another day and it couldn't turn out to be worse than this one.

THE END

FIGHTING RAMROD
Charles N. Heckelmann

Most men would have cut their losses, but Frazer counted the bullets in his guns and said he'd soak the range in blood before he'd give up another inch of what was his.

LONE GUN
Eric Allen

Smoke Blackbird had been away too long. The Lequires had seized the Blackbird farm, forcing the Indians and settlers off, and no one seemed willing to fight! He had to fight alone.

THE THIRD RIDER
Barry Cord

Mel Rawlins wasn't going to let anything stand in his way. His father was murdered, his two brothers gone. Now Mel rode for vengeance.

ARIZONA DRIFTERS
W. C. Tuttle

When drifting Dutton and Lonnie Steelman decide to become partners they find that they have a common enemy in the formidable Thurston brothers.

TOMBSTONE
Matt Braun

Wells Fargo paid Luke Starbuck to outgun the silver-thieving stagecoach gang at Tombstone. Before long Luke can see the only thing bearing fruit in this eldorado will be the gallows tree.

HIGH BORDER RIDERS
Lee Floren

Buckshot McKee and Tortilla Joe cut the trail of a border tough who was running Mexican beef into Texas. They stopped the smuggler in his tracks.

BRETT RANDALL, GAMBLER
E. B. Mann

Larry Day had the choice of running away from the law or of assuming a dead man's place. No matter what he decided he was bound to end up dead.

THE GUNSHARP
William R. Cox

The Eggerleys weren't very smart. They trained their sights on Will Carney and Arizona's biggest blood bath began.

THE DEPUTY OF SAN RIANO
Lawrence A. Keating and
Al. P. Nelson

When a man fell dead from his horse, Ed Grant was spotted riding away from the scene. The deputy sheriff rode out after him and came up against everything from gunfire to dynamite.

FARGO: MASSACRE RIVER
John Benteen

The ambushers up ahead had now blocked the road. Fargo's convoy was a jumble, a perfect target for the insurgents' weapons!

SUNDANCE: DEATH IN THE LAVA
John Benteen

The Modoc's captured the wagon train and its cargo of gold. But now the halfbreed they called Sundance was going after it . . .

HARSH RECKONING
Phil Ketchum

Five years of keeping himself alive in a brutal prison had made Brand tough and careless about who he gunned down . . .

FARGO: PANAMA GOLD
John Benteen

With foreign money behind him, Buckner was going to destroy the Panama Canal before it could be completed. Fargo's job was to stop Buckner.

FARGO: THE SHARPSHOOTERS
John Benteen

The Canfield clan, thirty strong were raising hell in Texas. Fargo was tough enough to hold his own against the whole clan.

PISTOL LAW
Paul Evan Lehman

Lance Jones came back to Mustang for just one thing — revenge! Revenge on the people who had him thrown in jail.